PENGUIN BOOKS

THE GUILTY PARTY

Josie knows she has to fight for what she believes in—and she believes too strongly in the anti-nuclear cause to allow a new nuclear power station to become operative on her doorstep. Josie knows her father would have approved and supported her, but he's dead and the relatives she and her mother now live with have little sympathy with her.

When Josie is picked up by the local police for fly-posting it's only the beginning of what is to be a difficult time for Josie and all those around her. She won't give up her principles, whatever her boyfriend or family say. But when she is arrested during a demonstration outside the power station she has to decide whether she's strong enough to face going to prison for her beliefs.

Joan Lingard has written many novels for adults and young people, including the popular 'Maggie' books and the 'Kevin and Sadie' books. She was born in Edinburgh but grew up in Belfast, where she lived until she was eighteen. She has three grown-up children and now lives in Edinburgh with her Canadian husband.

Other books by Joan Lingard

The 'Kevin and Sadie' books:

The Twelfth Day of July
Across the Barricades
Into Exile
A Proper Place
Hostages to Fortune

The Guilty Party

JOAN LINGARD

To Nina,

best wishes,

Joan Lingard

Penguin Books

This book is dedicated to
my daughter Jenny
on whose experiences I have drawn

PENGUIN BOOKS

Published by the Penguin Group
27 Wrights Lane, London W8 5TZ, England
Viking Penguin Inc., 40 West 23rd Street, New York, New York 10010, USA
Penguin Books Australia Ltd, Ringwood, Victoria, Australia
Penguin Books Canada Ltd, 2801 John Street, Markham, Ontario, Canada L3R 1B4
Penguin Books (NZ) Ltd, 182–190 Wairau Road, Auckland 10, New Zealand

Penguin Books Ltd, Registered Offices: Harmondsworth, Middlesex, England

First published by Hamish Hamilton Children's books 1987
Published in Penguin Books 1989
1 3 5 7 9 10 8 6 4 2

Printed and bound in Great Britain by
Cox & Wyman Ltd, Reading
Filmset in Baskerville

One

It began to look as if the paste might run out.

"No, I think we'll be all right," said Josie, peering into the plastic carrier bag which contained the pot. "We've only another half-dozen to do."

"Haven't we done enough?" asked Emma, who had had a sore head and a sore throat even before they set out. The last hour had not helped the headache: she had found it nerve-wracking, strolling around the town, trying to look 'nonchalant', as Josie put it, talking animatedly to one another whenever they saw, or thought they saw, a policeman. They had selected their targets beforehand, had known exactly which streets they were making for, and then, when the coast had seemed clear, or clear enough, they had acted quickly.

"Let's see it through." Josie was unrolling the next poster. She passed the carrier bag to Emma.

Emma went ahead. As she approached a billboard on her left, she took a brush from the bag and dipped it into the pot of glue; then, without breaking stride, she slashed it in wide strokes across the board. Coming behind, Josie placed the poster over the part that had been daubed. She lingered a moment to smooth out the wrinkles.

"Be quick!" called Emma, who had gone as far as the corner where she stood, on watch.

"I have to make sure it sticks." Josie pulled her head back to admire her handiwork. "Heavens, what a state my hands are in! And my cuffs! Me ma's going to do her nut when she sees me coat," she said, accentuating her Belfast accent.

"Car coming!" cried Emma.

Josie strolled over to join her.

"Nice night, isn't it?" she said. "Or it would be if the wind dropped."

The car was coming nearer. It had a blue light on its roof.

"Police," said Emma, unnecessarily, hunching her shoulders to control a shiver.

"Mary had a little lamb," said Josie. "Its fleas were white as snow . . ."

The police car drew level with them. It was cruising, seemed in no great hurry. Or else, it was interested in them. The girls did not look sideways.

"And everywhere that Mary went, the fleas were sure to go."

The car was past now, turning the corner into the next street.

"I think we should call it a night," said Emma. "I'm sure I'm getting 'flu."

"You go on home, Em, and get to your bed."

"You're not going to do any more, are you?"

"I might just slap the odd one up on the way back."

Be careful, warned Emma. Of course, said Josie, and they parted.

Josie walked slowly home, — or at least back to where she was living at present, for she would not have called it her home, — keeping a watchful eye on the street up ahead. Few people were about even though it was just gone ten; in this small English seaside town there would never be too many people about on an evening in late September. The summer visitors had scattered like leaves on the wind back to their city lairs and the town's residents appeared to go to their beds after they'd watched the nine o'clock news. She was a night bird herself, liked being awake while others slept.

She had been living in the town for only three months, though knew it well from holidays spent in it over the years, if holidays was the right word for the duty visits her parents had felt obliged to make to their relatives. But holidays were a different matter from everyday living and she had not yet adjusted to the change of tempo from life in Belfast. There were a number of things she had not yet adjusted to and she wondered if she ever would.

She saw a likely gable-end coming up. The wall of a corner shop where people would go in and out and maybe even stop to chat. And stopping, might look up and see the poster. It was an Asian shop. Khalil, the son of the owner, was in her form and sympathetic to the cause.

A quick glance round told her the street was empty. Working fast, but still taking care, she went through the procedure. Daub the wall with paste, unroll the poster, lift it up . . . As she was about to lay it against the wall, she heard the sound of the car. She turned. Headlights blazed and caught her full in the face.

"Is Josie in?" asked Rod, standing at the foot of the stairs with Josie's aunt, Mrs Oswald, close behind him. She had let him into the house. She wore a pink ribbed dressing gown and had her hair done up in spongy pink rollers. He had started to apologise for disturbing her so late, but she had cut him off, saying, "That's all right, son. I wasn't in my bed yet." She liked him, Josie had told him; she thought he came from a 'nice' family.

Mrs McCullough, Josie's mother, who must also have heard the bell, had come half way down the stairs. "I thought she'd gone to meet you, Rod? She left here at eight."

"I was supposed to meet her in the White Owl at ten."

"Ten?" said Mrs Oswald. "It's half eleven now."

"Where can she be?" said Mrs McCullough. She sounded anxious.

"Typical, isn't it?" said Mrs Oswald. "She's got no

consideration, that girl. She's probably gassing on some street corner."

"Not at *this* hour," said Mrs McCullough.

"She's no call to go worrying you after what you've been through. After what we've *all* been through."

"Oh God, what if something's happened to her?"

"Calm down now, Rona. Nothing'll have happened."

"But things *do* happen."

"Not here, Rona. This is a quiet town. This isn't Belfast, you know."

"Thank God for that," said Mr Oswald, who had just appeared in the hallway. He, too, was in a dressing gown, of brown and beige checks, with plaid slippers to match. "What's going on?" he demanded.

"It's Josie," said his wife. "She's stood up young Rod here — "

Rod cut in, suggesting they ring Emma, to see if she might know where Josie was.

Mrs Oswald thought it was far too late to ring a *doctor's* house, unless it was an emergency. "Hard working folk like them'll have been in their beds hours ago." But Mrs McCullough said they must ring. What else could they do? She couldn't just stand here waiting. She remembered the night when she'd waited for Josie's father to come home . . .

"There now, Rona." Mr Oswald patted her on the shoulder. "Don't be getting yourself worked up. Why don't you make her a wee cup of tea, Glad?"

His wife looked reluctant to go into the kitchen but did, leaving the door wide open so that she would miss nothing. It was a wonder she hadn't got her long thin nose trapped in a door before this, Josie had said to Rod; her Aunt Gladys was her father's half-sister and she had never known two people supposed to be related, who were less alike.

"Would you phone, Rod?" asked Mrs McCullough. "I don't feel like talking."

4

Rod dialled Emma's number and after it had rung a number of times, Emma's father answered. No, Josie was not there, he said, and Emma was asleep. "She's got a bad dose of 'flu. She came home about ten and went straight to bed. But look, if Josie doesn't turn up in the next half hour, ring back and I'll waken Emma."

Rod thanked Dr Hunter and replaced the receiver. Where could Josie be? Until now he had not been too worried, he had thought that possibly she had met someone, or was with Emma, and had forgotten the time. On his way along he had been getting really annoyed and was having a good going row with her in his head. Now all he could think of was that something bad might have happened to her and he felt sick inside.

Mrs Oswald brought the tea and Mrs McCullough sat on the bottom step to drink it.

"Now there's no bombers round here, Rona," said Mr Oswald, "so you can just relax."

"Your full name?"

"Josephine Rona McCullough."

"Age?"

"Seventeen."

"Address?"

She gave it. "Care of Oswald," she said. Care of. Who would want to be in the care of her Aunt Gladys and Uncle Frank? She and her mother had no option, not at the moment, not until their house in Belfast was sold, and that was not going to be easy. Right now they hadn't enough money to buy even a garden shed.

"Is that Oswald the ironmonger?"

"The very one."

"Are you lodging there or what?"

"Mrs Oswald's my aunt. My half-aunt."

"Which half?" asked the woman constable with a fleeting smile.

Josie gave an acknowledging grin. At least one of them had a sense of humour. The male constable didn't seem to have any. He was frowning.

"You're not from here, are you?" he asked. So far he had been sitting cleaning his nails with a match end.

"That's obvious, Jack," said his colleague.

"You Irish then?" He looked at Josie.

"Guilty, Your Honour."

"Just watch it." He threw the match end into the bin. "The station sergeant doesn't like cheek. He might decide to keep you in the cooler overnight."

"You've kept me waiting long enough as it is. My mother'll be worried sick about me."

"You should have thought of that before you decided to break the law, shouldn't you?"

"I hope I'm not keeping you back from anything important? Like hunting down terrorists or rapists."

"I warned you, didn't I?"

"Sorry," said Josie but did not drop her eyes. She felt as if the devil was in her tonight right enough, though she knew it would be better to be meek and mild. But meekness and mildness did not come naturally to her. The meek would inherit the earth, said her Uncle Frank, who was a pillar of the church. (He took up the collection on Sundays, afterwards discussing with his wife who had given what.) Josie did not believe it, about the meek and their possibilities of inheritance. Look round the world, she told her uncle; the men —and women — in power didn't look too meek to her. They seemed to have a fair conceit of themselves, as did the station sergeant, when he came sauntering in to see how things were going.

"Been in trouble before?" he asked, putting his face so close to hers that she smelt his thick, tobaccoey breath.

"I was once arrested for holding a candle on the steps of St. Martin's-in-the-Fields, in London."

"Oh, aye. Wee Willie Winkie, eh?"

"We were keeping a vigil." She'd been with her father and a couple of hundred others, protesting against Cruise missiles. They'd been brought to court later and fined. But the sergeant didn't seem to be interested.

"Irish eh? Belfast? Thought so. What are you doing over here?"

"Picking potatoes. When I'm not planting bombs."

"She's Frank Oswald's niece," said the male constable.

"Fancy that!"

"Do you think you could at least let them know where I am?" asked Josie.

"Were you aware," said the sergeant, "that by flyposting you were contravening a bye-law?"

"Will I get life, do you think?"

"Constable, let her cool her heels again for a little while."

When the constable arrived at the Oswalds' door, Josie's mother thought her heart would burst. She remembered again the night the policeman had come in Belfast. "Mrs Rona McCullough?" he had said. "I'm afraid I've got bad news . . ."

"It's all right, Rona," said Mr Oswald, stepping forward. "Leave this to me. What is it, Constable?"

"I've come on an identification check."

"*Identification*?" said Mrs McCullough and saw her daughter lying dead at the side of a road.

"Does Josephine Rona McCullough live here?"

"What's happened to her?" cried Mrs McCullough, pushing past her sister-in-law.

"Is this her address?"

"It is," said Mr Oswald.

"What is it?" said Mrs McCullough. "*Please* tell me!"

"She's been arrested — "

"Arrested?" cried Mrs Oswald and covered her mouth with her hand as if she would have liked to smother the word.

"What has she done?" asked her husband, in a quiet voice.

"She was flyposting."

"*Fly*posting?"

"Putting up posters on walls — "

Mrs McCullough began to laugh and went on laughing until the tears rolled down her cheeks. "I'm sorry," she said, sobering.

"You're hysterical," said her sister-in-law.

"No, no, just relieved. Flyposting!" And she began to laugh again.

"Are you holding her then, Constable?" asked Mr Oswald.

"She's at the station. The sergeant says if you come down, he'll release her into your charge."

Two

"The worst part," said Josie "was Uncle Frank coming to collect me. He looked as if he'd have liked to have dragged me along the gutter."

"He'd have a job dragging you, Josie!" said her friend Marge and they laughed, as did Emma, on whose bed they sat. Emma was still running a temperature and had been forbidden by her father to get up.

At five feet eight, Josie stood level with her Uncle Frank Oswald, shoulder to shoulder, eye to eye. Her UFO, she called him — or Unidentified Flying Object. He had flown at her once and struck her, when she was nine years old; for offering up cheek, he'd said. Her father had told him that if he were ever to lay a finger on her again it would be the last time he'd see any of them. With that thought in mind, she'd been tempted to have another go at provoking her uncle but her father had given her a strong warning too. He wasn't going to put up with her being cheeky to anyone, even if his brother-in-law could be somewhat trying, as he himself had been willing to acknowledge. "You've got to learn to control that devil in you, Josie!" She thought of her father now and sighed. Consciously changing her mood, she said:

"The UFO told me I was a right disgrace to him and Aunt Glad! 'We have to hold our heads up in this town, miss. We have to make a *living* in this town.' And the Glad Aunt moaned and held her head." Josie now adopted her aunt's voice. "'We're respected in this community. The shame of it — the police coming to our door! As if we were common criminals! And your uncle having to go to the police station and bail you out! She cheered up a bit when I told her they'd released me without charging me. I think she'd had visions of me featured in the *Weekly Gazette*. 'IRONMONGER'S NIECE CONVICTED.'"

"I feel I should own up too," said Emma. "It doesn't seem right that you should take all the blame. After all, there were six of us out altogether."

"More fool me then for getting caught," said Josie. She had known she was taking a risk when she'd done that last poster. And as for Emma *owning* up, this wasn't a school affair. *Hands up who stole the chalk or I'll keep the whole class in.* This was much more serious.

"It certainly is!" said Marge, who had been one of the six out flyposting.

"The police said I'd had a busy night," said Josie with a grin. They'd seen her down by the harbour and in the High Street. They'd been shadowing her and had known she hadn't been alone. "I told them they must have been seeing double."

"You really should watch what you say to them, Josie," said Emma. "We want to get them on our side, if we can. A lot of them probably are already."

"You're right, of course, Em," said Josie. Softly, softly, her father used to say: that's the best approach. He'd managed to do quite a lot himself by treading carefully but they'd got him in the end. "Next time — "

"Do you think there'll be a next time?" said Marge. "For getting arrested?"

"It's on the cards, isn't it? If we go ahead. And we must."

Josie and Marge left soon afterwards. Emma's mother saw them out.

"Emma was with you last night, wasn't she, Josie?" said Mrs Hunter. "Oh, you don't have to deny it, she told me so herself. I doubt if she'll be fit for Saturday, you know. But you can count on me."

"On *you*?"

"Oh yes, I'll be there. I've been on a few marches in my time — CND demonstrations and the like, and I wasn't sure what I felt about nuclear power when the public enquiry for our local plant was held ten years ago but I do now. Like a lot of other people."

"Since Chernobyl?"

"Since Chernobyl."

"What about Dr Hunter?" asked Marge.

"Oh, he's against it too, but he's not a man for demonstrations. He's a letter writer. He'll do what he can that way."

The two girls walked into the centre of town together. Marge was a head shorter than Josie, came up only to her shoulder. She was a skinny rabbit of a girl, said Aunt Gladys, who was not in favour of this friendship, disapproving as she did of the varying colours of Marge's hair, which currently was pink, and of Marge's family who, she claimed, were a pack of layabouts living off Social Security. Josie had exchanged a few sharp words with her aunt about that.

"Emma's lucky having her parents on her side in this," said Marge. "I daren't even let mine know what I'm up to. They'd go bananas. They'd see it as stabbing my dad in the back. He's hoping for work at the power station, you see. He's desperate for work. Well, I mean, he's been on the dole for two years."

"I can understand how he feels but what's the use of work if it could kill you in the end?"

"He doesn't see it that way."

"You should make him see it that way."

"It's easy enough talking."

"Oh, I know," said Josie, who was not having much success with that on her own home front. She had hardly been able to get a word in last night. Her aunt and uncle had sounded like a Greek chorus chanting a dirge.

11

"We're not wanting trouble."

"We want to live in peace."

Josie had jumped in there. "It might not be too peaceful if you have a nuclear accident on your doorstep."

"You know nothing about these things, madam," said Aunt Gladys. "Only what you read in the newspapers. And that's all exaggerated. Anything to sell papers."

"We're just wanting to lead a quiet life, Josephine," said Uncle Frank. "And you and your mother are welcome to stay as long as you keep yourselves quiet and peaceable too. It's the least we can do for David's memory."

"I've got to get out of the Oswalds' house", Josie said to Marge. "I'll have to look for a job." At present she worked, unpaid, for her uncle on Saturdays, as partial payment for the rent of their rooms.

Money was a problem for Marge too. She worked in kennels at week-ends, which she enjoyed — she wanted to be a vet — and two nights a week in a chip shop, which she hated. "It's the stink in my hair afterwards. I have to wash it three times to get rid of it."

They passed one of their posters on the side wall of a hotel which had closed for the winter. It looked a little scuffed but the words saying 'PROTEST MARCH TO NUCLEAR POWER STATION SITE, SATURDAY, LEAVING TOWN HALL 12 NOON', were still clearly legible.

"Will your uncle let you go on Saturday?" asked Marge. She had arranged to have the day off from the kennels.

"I wouldn't say he'll *let* me go. But I'll be there!"

They turned into the square and Josie hurried along to the White Owl cafe where she had arranged to meet Rod. The sight of his sandy fair head bent over his coffee cup gave her heart a lift. They'd only been going out together for nine weeks but she felt as if she'd known him half her life. Strange that. Perhaps it was because he, too, was a newcomer to the town. Or perhaps there was more to it than that.

"Sorry I'm late."

"That's all right."

They smiled at one another and Rod caught hold of her hand under the table and kept it.

"Sorry about last night too," she said. "For not turning up."

"Don't know if that's all right or not."

"Well, I know you won't approve — "

"Don't let's talk about it, Josie."

"Why not?"

"We've talked enough."

"No, we haven't." She took her hand away. "Not really talked. You refuse to talk about anything disturbing. It disturbs you because of your father, doesn't it?"

"No, it does not."

"You feel you've got to be on his side."

"It's not about *sides*. Why do you talk about everything as if it was a battle?"

"You'll be putting it down to my Irish background again. Maybe I can put your cussedness down to your Scottish one!"

"Do *we* have to fight, Josie?"

"I didn't come here to fight."

He was not looking at her any more, he was fiddling with the spoon in his saucer, and frowning. He was stubborn and difficult to budge, when he decided to close himself up, she knew him well enough to know that. She hated people closing themselves against her.

"You've made up your mind on this issue, haven't you," she said "and closed it? Tight, like a clam."

"You know where I stand, Josie."

"Yes, rooted to the spot." She stood up. "What's the point if we can't *talk*?" she said. And walked out.

Three

Rod watched Josie go. Let her go! he thought. To hell with her! He'd been looking forward to seeing her, had been thinking about her right through the afternoon, in Physics, and had been pulled up by the teacher for daydreaming. Why had Josie had to go and spoil it all? She was so damned headstrong! So argumentative. Why couldn't she ever let anything be?

Through the half-steamed up cafe window he saw her cross the road. He liked the way her dark shoulder-length hair swung back when she walked. He liked the way she walked, very straight-backed, taking a long stride. He never had to slow his pace when he walked with her. And he liked the bright colours that she wore. She loved colour: pinks that sizzled and oranges and lemons that made you think of sherbet and royal blue and emerald green. He liked to tease her saying he could always see her coming a mile off.

He pushed back his chair and got up. He went after her. When he was within hailing distance, he shouted, "Hey, you!"

She broke her stride and looked back. She hesitated for a moment. Then she stood and waited.

He stopped a yard or so from her. Their eyes met. They began to laugh and in the next instant had moved towards each other and had their arms round one another. They kissed, standing in the middle of the pavement, and the people going home from work had to circle round them.

"I'll be getting you a bad reputation in this town," said Josie when they separated. "You can be sure they'll blame it on me. That Irish hussey! Corrupting that nice Lawson boy."

They laughed, and with their arms round each other's waists, walked on.

"My mother thinks you're good for me," said Rod.

"Does she? And why would she think that?"

"I can't imagine," he said, though he could. His mother had thought he was inclined to spend too much time on his own, reading, working on models. Even back in Edinburgh, where he had had a number of close friends and a girlfriend too. But here he had been happy to be on his own much of the time, until he had met Josie.

"Do you want to come in for that biology book?" he said. She had to pass his house on her way home.

On the end wall of the Lawsons' street was a poster. "This one's for you, Mr Lawson," Josie had said at the time and Emma had said, "He's such a nice man. I wish he wasn't so nice." Niceness had nothing to do with it, Josie had retorted.

Rod brought her to a halt and read aloud from the small print at the bottom of the poster. "'Do you want your town turned into another Chernobyl? Do you want your children to run the risk of contracting leukaemia? If you are concerned, join us on our protest march . . .' A bit over the top, isn't it?"

"How can you say that?" she blazed. "Chernobyl *went* over the top, right over!"

"I know! It *was* terrible, I'm not trying to deny that, but this reactor's different."

"So *you* say!"

"Don't let's quarrel again! We've got to learn to agree to differ on this one."

"I find that difficult."

"I know you do. But why don't you try?"

She did not answer. They walked on to Rod's house.

It was a comfortable, stout, stone villa, surrounded by a large garden and a high stone wall. A house well-built to withstand the strong gales from the sea. It smelt of polish and

15

home baking. The Lawsons were so well settled in they might have lived there for a lifetime.

Mrs Lawson asked after Josie's mother. "She's had it hard, poor soul. I'm sure you must be a great support to her, dear. Would she like a loaf, do you think? I've just done a baking."

"I'm sure she'd love one."

The back door opened and in came Mr Lawson carrying his brief case. He smiled at Josie.

"I hear you're having a protest march on Saturday?"

"Nothing personal."

"I'm sure it isn't. You and I must have a good long talk though sometime, Josie."

"Josie likes to talk," said Rod. "And discuss things."

She wrinkled her nose at him.

"You know, Josie," said Mr Lawson, "the nuclear accident scare has got quite out of perspective. Have you ever thought about the accidents there have been in coal mines? Hundreds of men have died in the mines as well as from dreadful lung diseases. And what about Bhopal? *Twenty thousand* people died there. All industries carry risks, and the chemical ones, very high risks indeed."

"It's different though with nuclear power, isn't it? The after-effects of a nuclear accident go on for years and years."

"So will the after-effects at Bhopal."

"That shouldn't have been allowed to happen either!"

"This is not an ideal world. Accidents always will happen."

"Exactly! So nuclear accidents will happen too. We *could* have another Chernobyl down the road."

"It's extremely unlikely. It's a very safe reactor. Look, Josie, the world needs more energy. The Third World needs energy. We've got to upgrade our manufacturing industries, give people work. We're running out of fossil fuels."

"There are alternative sources of energy."

"They'd never come anywhere near fulfilling the world's requirements."

"How do we know when we haven't put enough money into researching them?"

"Is that not enough nuclear talk?" said Rod, who had been moving around restlessly in the background.

"What do you think, Mrs Lawson?" asked Josie, turning to her.

"I think we must trust the scientists and engineers, dear. They want to live too, you know. They don't want to run unnecessary risks. I trust Ben." And she looked at her husband.

It must make life simpler if you can think that way, thought Josie. The Hunters had also come originally from Scotland and Mrs Hunter had known Rod's mother, a long time ago. She said Mrs Lawson had been an awfully nice girl, with no strong opinions of her own, and now she was an awfully nice woman, with opinions taken from her husband.

"Why don't you come along to the power station and let me give you a tour?" said Mr Lawson. "See for yourself. What about tomorrow after school? Rod could bring you along."

"Very well," said Josie. She was willing.

"Come to supper afterwards," said Mrs Lawson.

Rod walked Josie to the corner. She didn't have to go to the power station, he said. It's all right, she said, she wanted to. "Leave me here, will you, Rod? I'd like to go the rest of the way alone. It's just that I haven't had a minute on my own all day and I need time to think."

They kissed and parted and came back to kiss again. They moved around the corner and leant against the wall. After a while, Josie said she really *must* go or else her mother would start worrying again. "And your supper will be burnt."

"I don't give a damn about my supper!"

Finally, they separated. Rod stood on the corner watching her until she was out of sight.

Josie emerged from the shelter of the town on to the open promenade. The wind was boisterous and took hold of her hair whipping it about her face. She laughed. She liked the feel of the wind and the smell of the sea and the sight of the white breakers crashing on the sand below. She liked to walk on the beach with Rod, though usually they ran, tugging one another along.

Too soon, she reached the row of terraced houses where her aunt and uncle lived. Her aunt was loitering in the lobby. She always loitered with intent. She beckoned to Josie with her forefinger. "A word," she said and led the way into the living room where her husband sat at the table eating liver and onions and watching the television news. She turned the sound down.

"We have something to say to you, Josephine. We are good Christian people and we didn't hesitate to take you and your mother in when your poor father got blown up by the IRA."

"We don't know it was the IRA! It could just as easily have been the UDA or UVF."

"Don't be talking blethers," said Uncle Frank, spearing a piece of liver on his fork. "Of course it was the IRA. Your father was a Protestant. Of sorts, anyway."

"Dad was running a youth club for both Protestants and Catholics. A few extremists on either side didn't like that but no one ever claimed responsibility so we don't *know* who did it."

"I knew no good would come from him setting up that youth club," said Aunt Gladys. "It was asking for trouble trying to mix the two lots together. Especially a crowd like that. Nothing but street corner yobs."

"You don't know what they were like," said Josie, rounding

on her. "You haven't been over in Belfast in years, have you?" Scared to death to come, she'd have liked to add, but even she knew there were limits. As long as she was under the Oswalds' roof. "At least Dad tried to *do* something, instead of sitting lamenting."

Uncle Frank washed down the last of the liver with a mouthful of tea. "Josie, what we want to say to you is this— we don't want you to go out on that protest business on Saturday morning. If you do, I'm afraid we'll have to ask you to leave our house."

"It's only a march! We're not going to break the law. What are you so afraid of?"

"Watch how you talk to us, girl!" said Aunt Gladys. "We don't care for you to be associated with the kind of rabble that goes on these marches. They attract all sorts of riff-raff. Most of them look as if they haven't had a bath in months. Like those women at Greenham Common."

"What's that?" said Josie, pointing suddenly at the flickering television screen. "Looks like a Loyalist march to me." There were Union Jacks waving in the breeze and banners depicting King Billy on his white horse and pipes and drums could be seen even though they could not be heard.

"That's different," said Aunt Gladys. Her father — and Josie's grandfather — had been an Orangeman. "It's traditional for them to parade. Anyway, they're showing their loyalty to the Crown."

"Oh, is that what they're doing?"

"Think it over," said Uncle Frank, as Josie made for the door. "And remember a roof over your head's not so easy come by. Remember your mother, too, for she's had enough to cope with already."

"We have our standards," said Aunt Gladys. "And we don't see why you should lower them."

Josie looked back from the door. "You might be interested

to know that Mrs Hunter — the *doctor's* wife — will be amongst the unwashed rabble!"

She resisted the temptation to slam the door behind her, just. Outside in the hallway, she fumed and wondered that smoke was not rising from the top of her head. She was certainly not going to give in to that blackmail!

"Is that you, love?" came her mother's voice from overhead.

Josie climbed the stairs to the second floor where she and her mother had two attic rooms and a cupboard that served as a kitchen. They shared the bathroom on the first floor with the Oswalds. Once upon a time Mrs McCullough had lived in the house next door with her parents, both of whom were now dead. She had met her husband when he had been on a visit to his sister.

"I wish we didn't have to stay here," said Josie.

"Where else can we go?"

After they'd eaten, they sat by the gas fire drinking coffee.

"Josie," began her mother.

"Yes?"

Mrs McCullough sighed. "I hate having to ask you this — "

"Must you then?"

"I'm afraid so."

"You don't want me to go on Saturday, that's it, isn't it?"

"We need these rooms."

"I'll leave school and get a job and we'll rent some rooms."

"I want you to finish school. I want you to go to university. Your father would have wanted it too."

"But he'd be out there protesting himself, you know that!"

"I know, I know!" said Mrs McCullough and her voice sounded close to breaking. Josie left her chair to come and kneel beside her. She put her arm round her mother.

"Mum, I can't let the others down."

"I don't know if I can take any more, Josie. Not at the

moment. I could be doing with a bit of peace. For years I lived with the worry that something would happen to your father. He would never stay back in any situation. Well, you know that. He believed you should commit yourself to what you believed in, and I admired him for that, but I worried myself sick at the same time. And now you — "

"It's not quite the same, Mum."

"I can't face the thought of living in some squalid wee room either."

It wouldn't come to that, said Josie. "The Oswalds might turn me out but they'll hardly put you on the street."

"And do you think I'd let you go alone?" said her mother. "Josie, *please*, don't go on Saturday. For my sake."

Four

When they had cleared up, Josie went for a walk along the promenade. She walked up and down, up and down, with her hands plunged deep in her pockets and her collar pulled up against the wind's bite, and once more allowed the arguments which had plagued her all day to rage inside her head.

What was she to do? She was one of the march's organisers. Could she let them down? But if she did go, what then? She wouldn't mind being put out in the street. They'd find a room somewhere, she and her mother, even if it was only a boxroom. She'd rather sleep on the floor than stay in her relatives' house under sufferance. The UFO had seen her on her way out. "Off out *again*?" he'd said. She was sure that they sat in their living room with their door ajar so that they would miss none of her comings and goings.

Her mother, though, would not want to sleep on a floor or in some damp boxroom with only a skylight for a window. And why should she? They had so little money, so little choice. It would take ages to get a council house even if they were to put their name down straight away. Josie sighed. She had to think of her mother.

She stopped at the point where the houses ran out and leant on the sea wall facing the sea.

"Are you all right?"

Spinning round, she saw a woman in a red coat. The light here was feeble and for a moment she did not recognise the constable who had questioned her at the police station the night before.

"I'm fine," she said warily even though the woman appeared to be off duty.

"This is a lonely place to be hanging about in at night."

"I can take care of myself. I've done a self-defence course."

"I'll need to watch myself then eh?" They laughed. The woman hesitated, then, coming a step closer, said in a voice so low that Josie only just caught the words above the sound of the sea, "If I wasn't in the police I'd be with you on Saturday. But that's between you and me, of course."

"Of course," said Josie.

The policewoman in the red coat said goodnight and continued along the promenade towards the town. Josie resumed her patrol.

To go or not to go? That, indeed, was the question! And reminded her that she should be at home reading Hamlet for she had an English essay to hand in the next morning. Hamlet had been a ditherer but no one had ever accused her of that. She was usually accused of acting too impetuously. This case, however, was different. She was torn two ways, and whichever one she chose, her conscience would trouble her.

What would her father have said if he were here? She knew he would approve of the cause — there was no doubt about that, for he had been deeply troubled by all the things that man was doing to despoil the earth, and he would approve of her being involved in the cause — but she knew, too, that he would expect her to put her mother first.

"She's suffered enough, Josie." She thought she heard his voice but when she listened again she heard only the swish of the sea and the moan of the wind.

The march would go on even if she was not there.

On her way home she met Jack Dempster, Marge's boyfriend. He was excited. Lots of people were coming on Saturday, he said. "They keep stopping me and telling me we've got their support. Of course I can't really see who'd be for the power station, can you?"

"Oh, I don't know. Rod is, after all. And his father."

"That's because Mr Lawson's one of the senior engineers. I hear the construction workers will be working on Saturday afternoon so I think we should blockade the gate, don't you?"

"Probably."

"Are you O.K.? Not getting 'flu too, are you? We can't do without you."

"No, I'm fine. Just tired."

"Not like you to be tired, Josie."

"Everybody's tired at times, Jack."

As she trudged the rest of the way home, she felt that her legs moved like sandbags beneath her. She wanted to fall into bed and sleep for hours.

Her mother was in her room reading.

"I'm not going to go on Saturday, Mum", said Josie.

Neither she nor her mother slept well that night. They did not talk much over breakfast but before she left for school Josie said she wouldn't be coming straight home in the afternoon.

"You don't mind?"

"Of course not." Her mother spoke in an automatic way, without looking up. She was sitting in her dressing gown with her elbows on the table and her head propped between her hands staring into her empty coffee cup. Josie wondered if she would go back to bed once she was out of the door. Before her father died her mother had been active, always on the go; she had worked full-time as a physiotherapist, gone out in the evenings to the theatre and the cinema and to visit friends. Here, she had no friends, apart from her relatives, for most of her old schoolfriends had moved away, and although she'd made one or two half-hearted enquiries about a job there didn't seem to be much prospect of her finding one.

"I don't have to go to the Lawsons for supper, Mum. I could come home."

Her mother lifted her head. "Don't be silly, of course you must go."

"But I hate you being on your own so much."

"On you go to school or you'll be late. I'll be all right. I've got a dental appointment this afternoon and I'm going to go to the launderette in the morning." Mrs McCullough made an attempt to smile.

"Oh, Mum!" Josie threw down her books and rushed back to her. She put her arms around her mother and held her, rocking her a little, as her mother used to do to her when she was younger and upset. "Perhaps we shouldn't have left Belfast."

"It seemed like a good idea at the time, to get away."

"We can always go back."

"Well, we'll see. Now go, love, or you really will be late! And don't worry about me!"

They were always telling each other not to worry about one another.

Josie picked up her books and ran. She felt guilty when she left her mother alone for any length of time. And she felt guilty, too, that she was going to have to tell her friends that she wouldn't be there to support them on Saturday morning. When the idea had been hers in the first place!

Rod was waiting at his corner for her. "You're late," he said. "You're always late."

"So would you be if you'd my life to lead. You should have gone on."

"I waited, didn't I?" He took her free hand.

Let's not go to school, she was tempted to say, let's go away somewhere for the day. Let's forget about your family and my family, about nuclear power, and arguments for and against, and about Hamlet and Ophelia! (Her essay was pathetic, had been scrawled at midnight, and if the teacher threw it back at her she wouldn't blame him.) Rod might go, if she talked him into it, but it would just cause more trouble, with everybody.

"We'd better run," she said.

At lunchtime Josie and Marge paid Emma a quick visit and Josie told them that she wouldn't be able to go on the march on Saturday.

"Oh well," said Marge. "You've got to have a roof over your heads, haven't you?"

"If you ever are put out," said Emma, "you can come here."

Josie thanked her whilst knowing that whereas it might be possible to take up the offer for a night or two, she and her mother could not stay any longer. There were four children in the Hunter family as it was.

"It must be great to have *control* over your life, mustn't it?" said Marge.

It must, Josie agreed fervently. Last night, lying awake listening to the wind howling round the roof, she had considered the ways in which that might be achieved and had come to the conclusion that the only answer was to earn some money.

"You could always get a job at the plant," said Marge.

"Sweeping up the nuclear waste!" said Josie and they laughed, all three.

There wasn't much sign of waste of any kind at the power station. Everything was immaculately clean. Tubes, pipes, boilers, turbogenerators, fuel pins, the white coats of the workers, all gleamed with newness and brightness. Of course the plant hadn't gone into operation yet.

"But even when we do go operative," said Mr Lawson, "it will still be very clean. That's one of its big advantages."

"Unless you have an accident," said Josie, readjusting her hard hat which was a little on the large side.

"As I keep telling you, Josie, the chances are very very

26

small. All the systems are fail safe. For every fault condition that *could* happen there are two lines of protection. It's not a case of one man making a mistake."

"But you could get a succession of human errors."

"If one single mistake is made, no matter how small, then the system is tripped and the reactor shuts down automatically and it can't be switched on without a full investigation from the Nuclear Installations Inspectorate. It's not like stalling a car and switching the engine back on."

Rod had moved away from them to have another look at the turbines.

"But they must have had fail safe systems at Chernobyl and Three Mile Island," said Josie.

"The kind of accident that happened at Chernobyl simply could not happen here," said Mr Lawson and she could take his word for that. "The risks have been reduced to vanishing point."

Can he believe that? she wondered. Can there ever be no risk at all when people have to operate the controls? They seemed to be on either side of a high fence, she and Rod's father, with no possibility of either of them scaling it. She believed that he believed what he was saying, but she could not believe it.

She could not take in the complexity of everything that he was telling her, could not hope to. She was impressed by the skill and sophistication of the engineering, felt slightly dazed by the immensity of it all, though she understood vaguely how it worked. She had grasped the fact that heat was transferred from nuclear fission to the boilers by a coolant gas and then the steam which was produced in the boilers supplied the turbines which drove the generators. They had walked from building to building looking at the giant pipes and machines and she had even been able to admire them, as pieces of machinery. She could understand someone wanting to be an

27

engineer. Though not a nuclear engineer.

"Let's go to the control room," said Mr Lawson.

It was a large room, housing a central island of switches and visual display units, with other control panels all round the walls. It made her think of a James Bond film. She could imagine terrorists rushing in and throwing the switches. Mr Lawson laughed.

"They wouldn't get this far without tripping the alarm systems."

"But what if one of the engineers went berserk?"

"There are never less than three on duty at any time. The other two could over-ride anything he did. The reactor would just shut down. You see, Josie, we *have* thought of everything."

They went up to Mr Lawson's office for coffee and he produced a bar of brazil nut chocolate. He offered Josie a piece which she accepted.

"Do you like brazil nuts?"

"Love them. They're my favourite nuts."

"Did you know that they're highly radioactive?"

Josie stopped chewing, not because the idea of the radioactivity of the nuts put her off, but because she suspected that the chocolate had been deliberately bought and given to her to make a point.

"They're twenty thousand times more radioactive than baked beans," said Mr Lawson.

For a moment she was nonplussed, and wondered that the chocolate bar was not vibrating in her hand. Then she told herself, Don't be bamboozled, use your loaf! She said slowly, "But you couldn't get a lethal dose of radioactivity from eating brazil nuts, could you? I mean, you'd choke to death on them long before you reached that point."

"True," he conceded. So she had won a point! "But there's radioactivity even in our houses — it comes from the insulation."

"Mr Lawson, I *know* we have to live with a certain amount of radioactivity in our lives — "

"What I'm trying to make you realise that radioactivity in reasonable amounts is not all that bad."

"It's not the reasonable amounts I'm worried about."

"I think we should be going," said Rod. "Mum'll have supper ready."

They went back down to Reception, handed in their hats and walked across the site through the two security fences to the entrance gate. Josie was glad of the fresh air. She had a slight headache. The security man checked them out.

As they were getting into the car Mr Lawson said, "So what do you think now, Josie?"

"Well, I *am* impressed by the engineering and all that and I can see that the safety standards *are* very high but if there is even the smallest chance of an accident then it seems to me to be too high a price to pay. And then there is the question of nuclear waste — "

"Shouldn't we be getting home?" said Rod impatiently.

He walked her home later and they talked about travelling. Perhaps, they said, we might go away next summer, together. They could travel around Europe, go for the whole summer, take a tent, maybe even cycle, live cheaply . . . It would be nice, they said, let's try for that. It would be something to look forward to throughout the winter, said Rod, throughout the long slog for A levels. Josie wondered how she would be able to leave her mother for a whole summer when it was difficult enough to leave her for an evening, but she did not say so to Rod.

Standing outside the Oswalds' gate, they discussed which countries they would visit. Austria, said Rod, and Switzerland. He liked mountainous countries. France, said Josie, and Italy; oh, and Greece, too, she must go to Greece. Why stop there?

said Rod, they might as well go on to Turkey.

"Is that you, Josephine?" said a voice from the porch.

"No, it's an imposter," she said softly, "in Josie clothing."

"Will you be coming in then?" said Uncle Frank. "I'm waiting to lock up for the night."

Her mother's light was still on. Josie had half hoped she might have gone to bed and felt guilty that she had even had the thought. She seemed to feel guilty half the time at present, about something or other. That would be because she had plenty to feel guilty about, the UFO would say, if he could hear her thinking. Her thoughts seemed to be the only place she could keep private from him.

She was surprised to see her mother looking brighter and more cheerful than she had in the morning.

"Josie," said Mrs McCullough straight away, "you're to go on the march on Saturday."

Josie stared at her.

"I mean it! I should never have asked you not to."

Five

"I realised it was selfish of me," said Mrs McCullough, "as soon as you'd gone out this morning. You're doing what you believe to be right, after all, and, what's more, *I* believe it to be right too."

"Are you sure, Mum?"

"Absolutely."

Josie was amazed by the change in her mother. She sounded more like the woman she used to be

"Another thing I realised, Josie, was that I'd need to *do* something. I couldn't sit up here in this attic feeling sorry for myself much longer. I'd be letting down your father's memory if I did."

"But, Mum, it was understandable."

"Maybe it was. But life has to go on."

"So what have you done?" asked Josie, for it was clear that her mother must have done something.

"Well, I got talking to the dentist, telling him how I would like to find work — "

"And he offered you a job?"

"Not quite. But he did offer me a room in his house so that I could set up as a physiotherapist. He says he'll recommend me to his patients and then I can advertise too."

"Fantastic!"

Josie leapt up to hug her mother, who protested, laughing, saying Josie would crush her with that bear hug, saying not to get carried away too soon, she didn't have one patient yet. But she was optimistic that she soon would. Yes, she was optimistic. For the first time in months.

"But what about me going on the march, Mum, and us getting thrown out?"

"I'm not so worried about that now. We'll cope with it if we have to but I doubt it'll come to that. I know the Oswalds bark a lot but I'm not sure they've got the nerve to bite."

As the days went by, bringing Saturday closer, excitement mounted amongst the march organisers. They held meetings every day, perhaps more than they needed for organisational purposes, but they did have a need to be together. And, as they said to one another, they must know exactly what their strategy was going to be, and what they would do when they reached the gates of the site. Someone would have to make a speech, for one thing.

"You can do that, Josie," said one of the boys, Phil Peters. "It's right up your street."

She began to protest but Marge interrupted saying, "Oh, go on, you've got the gift of the gab!"

"Thanks a million," said Josie, but, in fact, she didn't mind the idea of speaking in public.

"Hey, you could become an M.P.," said Marge. "This'll be good practice."

"You never know the day!" said Josie with a smile.

"Which party?" asked Emma.

"Oh, *no* party. I'll be an Independent."

There was something else to be decided, said Jack, and that was whether they should take any action that was outside the law, like going over the fence or lying down in the road.

"I don't see what that would achieve", said Emma.

"It would attract attention from the media," said Phil.

"Only for a few minutes," said Khalil.

"But if we go meekly home like lambs," said Josie, "then they'll think that's fine, they've had their little demonstration and now we can get on with the work on hand. We've got to show that our opposition is stronger than that."

They were split on the issue, roughly fifty-fifty. In the end it was decided that those who wished to lie down in the road and blockade the site should do so and those who did not should be equally free not to do so without the others resenting it.

"If we do lie down we'll get arrested, of course," said Jack. "We have to be prepared for that."

On Friday evening, Rod wanted Josie to go with him to see a film.

"I'm sorry, Rod, I'd love to, really I would, but — "

"You've got a meeting!"

"We've got to finalise arrangements for tomorrow."

"I've hardly seen you this week. Except in the mornings on the way to school and then half the time we have to run because you're late."

"You could always come to the meeting with me," said Josie, tongue in cheek.

He didn't answer. He shrugged, kicked a stone into the gutter.

"Couldn't you?" she said, unable to resist pushing a little further.

"No," he said shortly.

They walked a way in silence with a stretch of pavement between them. He had his head down and his lips pursed. Let him sulk, she thought. It was his fault anyway — it was he who chose to stay outside. Gradually, she had been finding that people at school were falling into two groups, of us and them. Those who were for us and those who were against. The issue was dividing the town.

"You're getting obsessed with this damned business," said Rod.

Her temper rose then. "It's a matter of life and death!"

"Now you're getting hysterical."

"Oh, am I indeed? It's a wonder you want to waste your time with me then, isn't it?"

"Yes, it is," he said and went swerving off down a side street.

She walked straight on and she didn't look back. She marched up the hill to Marge's house and went round to the back door.

Marge's mother opened it. "Oh, it's you, Josie." She sounded less welcoming than usual, Josie thought, though wondered if she was beginning to imagine things. But often Mrs Gibson would call her 'love' or 'dear' and stop what she was doing to have a bit of a crack. Today, without another word, she went back to the ironing board which she must have left to come and answer the door. She lifted a shirt and spread it over the board. The steam iron hissed as she pushed it along.

"How are you the day?" asked Josie.

"Oh, all right," said Mrs Gibson, not sounding it.

"Marge in?"

"She's upstairs."

Marge was sitting at the card table in her room writing up biology notes. Josie plonked herself down on the bed.

"I hate Roderick Lawson," she declared.

"Oh?"

"We've split. I'm finished with him."

"I bet you were arguing about the plant? What a lot of trouble it's causing." said Marge gloomily.

"Marge, *you're* not going to drop out!"

"Of course not. What do you take me for? I'm not as lily-livered as that. No, but my mum knows and she isn't pleased. She's not at all pleased. Dad heard this morning he's got a job there, you see, driving a truck."

"Oh no!"

"Oh yes!" said Marge.

As Josie busied herself around her uncle's hardware shop she hummed, under her breath, her mind on the march and not on the packets of thumb tacks and tins of paint stripper that she was setting to rights. At the far end of the shop, the UFO sat behind the counter in his fawn coat doing the accounts. He had wanted her to wear an overall, too, but she had drawn the line at that. She hated overalls and she hated the colour fawn, if it could be called a colour at all. This morning she was wearing a scarlet jersey and green corduroy trousers. *Red and green should never be seen, except on the back of an Irish queen.* The jingle ran through her head making her smile.

"Time to open up," said Uncle Frank, lifting his head.

She unbolted the door and went out on to the pavement for a minute. The sun dazzled her eyes. The forecast though had talked of showers in the afternoon.

When she went back inside her uncle said, "I'm glad you've decided to be sensible, Josephine." She said nothing.

The door pinged open announcing the first customer of the day. It was Rod's father.

"Ah, good morning, Mr Lawson," said Uncle Frank, who had come shooting down the aisle as soon as he saw who the customer was. Josie hated the way he toadied to any of the customers whom he thought were 'better' than he was. She left them to have a discussion about emulsion paint for the Lawsons' bathroom.

"Cheerio, Josie," Mr Lawson called over to her, when he'd got his parcel made up. "Sorry I can't wish you luck on the march today!"

"Oh, she's going on no march," said Uncle Frank.

"She's not?"

"No, Mr Lawson, she is not. She's come to her senses, I'm glad to say."

Shortly after eleven o'clock, Marge arrived looking as if she hadn't slept. Josie led her round behind a rack of saucepans.

"Guess what? My dad started work this morning! Somebody took ill and they needed a replacement straight away."

"Josephine!" called Mr Oswald, who had been squinting at them through the gaps between the saucepans. "Customer." A woman was just coming in.

"He could serve her himself," muttered Josie. "Stupid ould UFO git! Wait there, Marge!"

The woman wanted a packet of brillo pads. As Josie was serving her she heard her uncle say to Marge, "Can I help you?" and Marge say, "No, it's all right, thanks. I'm waiting to speak to Josie." "She's busy." "I'll just wait."

When the customer had gone Josie rejoined Marge. Her uncle continued to hover nearby like a large fawn moth. Josie wished she could brush him aside. Or swipe him with one of the fly swats. The thought made her want to giggle. The girls moved up towards the entrance together; he followed. Josie escorted Marge out on to the pavement.

"Don't feel you've got to come on the march. Not if it's going to cause too much trouble for you at home."

"I don't know what to do." Marge scuffed the edge of the kerb with her toe.

"Josephine!" came the call from within.

"Oh, drop dead! I'd better go back in. Maybe see you later, Marge?"

"Maybe. I'll need to think."

"There's too much work to be done for you to stand chatting to your friends." Mr Oswald began, but Josie walked past him and through the back shop and into the toilet, where she locked the door and stood with her back to it, her arms folded. She'd need the patience of a saint to put up with him, and she was a long way from sainthood. She opened the window and peered out into the back lane. A ginger cat was crawling along the wall stalking something she couldn't see. She envied it its freedom.

Fifteen minutes later, her mother arrived. She took off her coat and parked her handbag behind the counter. Mr Oswald stared at her.

"I've come to take over from Josie, Frank."

"How do you mean like?"

"I'm relieving her for the rest of the day."

"Relieving her?"

"Yes, she's got to be at the town hall at twelve o'clock."

Six

"You should have seen the UFO's face!" said Josie to Emma, who was standing, looking a little white-faced, in a huddle with some others outside the town hall. "I thought he was going to go into orbit."

"But he didn't try to stop you?"

"How could he?"

"On you go then," Mrs McCullough had said, and Josie had gone, running, closing the door on the raised voices of her mother and uncle.

More people were arriving, but there was no sign as yet of Marge. Josie waved to her history teacher, Mr Greig. He had his wife with him, and their two young children, one walking, the other in a push-chair, and they were talking to another couple with three children. The husband of the second family held up a poster on which was written :
WE WANT A SAFE FUTURE FOR OUR CHILDREN.

The organisers all carried posters. The slogans, printed in bright colours — orange and red and green — varied slightly but carried the same message.

DON'T FORGET CHERNOBYL

IT COULD HAPPEN HERE

WE WANT A SAY IN OUR FUTURE

WE WANT A FUTURE

WE SAY NO TO NUCLEAR POWER

"There's Mum," said Emma, waving, "with her friend Mrs Harman. And there's the vicar!"

"Pity the UFO and the Glad Aunt aren't here to see that," said Josie. "Wait till I tell them!"

38

"Here comes the law!" said Phil.

They turned to see a police van drawing up. Out of the back clambered a number of constables — ten in all — in mackintoshes and helmets and carrying walkie-talkies. They were in the charge of a sergeant, the one whom Josie had encountered on the night of her arrest. He had in his hand a loud hailer. At the moment that she saw him, he saw her and his eyes, which had been roving over the faces in the crowd, stopped on hers and rested there, for fully thirty seconds.

"Probably got me down as an urban terrorist," said Josie. "I heard that's how they class the women at Greenham. I'm sure my friend the Serge thinks I'm in the IRA."

"Now be careful, Josie!" said Emma. "We've agreed — no aggro — even if we get it from them. There'd be nothing to be gained by it."

"I know, I know!" Josie had given herself a lecture in bed that morning, all to do with keeping the head and self-control in general.

"It's ten past," said Jack, scanning the late comers who were still straggling into the square. "Looks like Marge isn't going to make it."

"Hey, we've just topped a thousand!" said Khalil, clicking the calculator in his hand. He had been given the job of keeping a tally.

That delighted them for they knew that for every person who did come out there would be another ten or a hundred or even a thousand at home who either could not or would not come on a demonstration, but were with them in spirit. Like Dr Hunter, writing letters (though Josie couldn't help thinking it might have been better if he'd just come; he could write letters any time), or Jack's granny who would have been with them if she hadn't needed a zimmer to get around. The rest of Jack's family — mother, father, brother, sister — was in the crowd. Jack's father was a fireman. He said he didn't fancy sacrificing himself fighting a fire in a nuclear reactor.

"I think we'd better start, don't you?" said Josie and Jack nodded. They couldn't wait any longer for Marge. Together, Phil and Josie raised the main banner, each taking one pole. The scarlet words rippled in the breeze:
WE SAY NO TO NUCLEAR POWER.

The sergeant came striding towards them. "No more than four abreast! We don't want the road blocked. The traffic's got to keep moving too."

They began to move forward, Josie and Phil leading the way, flanked by Emma and Jack. Khali stayed by the side of the road so that he could continue with his calculations. The crowd thinned out to form a long snake weaving through the streets of the town. The police spaced themselves out and walked beside the procession, the sergeant remaining at the front. A few people with guitars began to tune up.

Some women waved to them from the pavement and called out, "We're with you", but another shouted, "Our men need the jobs", and one man, as they were passing, spat, and his spittle landed on Emma's leg. Emma shuddered and scrubbed the stain off her jeans with a tissue.

"Fifthy pig!" said Josie who, if she had not been carrying the banner, would have run after the man. "It's a pity he didn't spit a bit further." She nodded at the sergeant's stiff back.

"Shush now," said Emma.

They turned into the street where Mr Oswald had his hardware shop. As they drew level, Josie looked sideways, and there he was, at the back of the door, peeping around the OPEN sign. She waved and the fawn coat shrank back, out of view, but not before she'd caught sight of the look on his face. There was going to be the devil to pay when she got back!

They came to the edge of the town and were now in open country. The trees shone, red, orange and gold, in the bright sunshine. The air smelt fresh and clean. It was difficult to imagine that it could ever become polluted, Josie thought, as she shifted the pole a little to ease the pressure on her right arm. So polluted that anyone breathing it in might afterwards become sick and die, as they had done at Hiroshima. Or at Chernobyl.

It would have been a good day to have gone for a long walk, over the fields, or beside the sea, as she and Rod had done the previous Saturday. They had gathered shells and spun smooth flat pebbles through the waves. And had walked barefoot on the sand leaving their prints behind them. They had walked with their arms around one another's waists. She wondered what Rod would be doing this afternoon.

He was building a bonfire in his back garden. He had swept the dry leaves up from the paths and pruned the rose bushes and put the chopped-off stems on to the pile. In the spring he planned to start a rock garden. He liked gardening. It quietened him when he felt restless. He felt restless this afternoon.

He was wondering how the march was getting on. From the attic window he had seen it pass two streets below and through the open window had caught the odd snatch of music. The town seemed very quiet though he knew that most people could not be out marching. They were probably sitting at home in front of their telly sets watching Saturday Grandstand!

He was wondering how Josie was getting on. He could imagine her striding out, black hair flying, ready for anything. She was an idiot that girl, so hot-headed! He hoped she wouldn't do anything daft and get arrested again. "You'd never do anything really daft, would you, Rod?" she'd said to him once, and her words had stayed with him, squirming around inside his head, like softly-moving coiled snakes. Was it true? And if it was, did it matter? He was not sure. He had a quick temper, like her, but once it had flared it died as quickly as it had risen and he seldom did anything rash in the heat of it. Though he *had* walked away from her yesterday. Just as well, they were so different. Too different for comfort. The ten weeks with her had been anything but comfortable. He smiled at the idea.

Striking a match, he watched the flame catch on the edge of a curled up leaf. Within seconds fire was crackling and streaking through the pile of leaves and sticks. It had been a bit like that when he had first met Josie. They had caught alight quickly, and all of a sudden, and it had left them both slightly breathless. There had been no time to consider whether they were suited or not.

She had excited him, from the moment they had collided in the school playground in the middle of a game of impromptu football. She'd been running for the ball and had landed smack up against him. He'd put out his arms to catch her and she'd swayed back and stopped and looked him full in the face. By then someone else had got the ball and the play had moved away. They had been left standing.

From then on he had wanted to be with her all the time. He still did! He could not deny it.

"That's a good fire, Rod," said his father, coming up behind him. He squatted on the greenhouse step and together they watched the soft white smoke rise up into the still air.

"Josie gone on the walk?"

"I expect so."

"Her uncle said she wasn't going. But I hardly think I managed to change her mind, do you?"

"No," said Rod and heaped more leaves on to his fire. The centre of it was glowing hot.

"She's a bright girl. But over-reacting to the whole accident possibility, you know. Got it all out of proportion."

"I don't want to talk about it any more," said Rod.

"All right! I do like her, you know. A lot. So do you, it seems. You're pretty close, aren't you?"

Rod lifted one shoulder in a shrug and bent over the fire. He did not want to discuss Josie with his father. He did not want to discuss her with anybody.

"Not very communicative this afternoon, are you?" His father gave him a wry smile.

"Sorry."

"Not to worry. I'll see you later, Rod." Mr Lawson went back into the house.

Rod stamped out the embers of the fire and taking his bicycle from the shed cycled down into the centre of town, going nowhere in particular, he told himself, but found that he was turning into the street where Josie's uncle kept his shop. The CLOSED sign was up on the door; they must be shut for lunch. The sight of the sign depressed him. It was a beautiful afternoon but he didn't know what to do with it.

As the march progressed, yet more people tacked on to the back, keeping Khalil's finger clicking. They sang, everything from *Tipperary* to *We Will Overcome* and *Old MacDonald Had a Farm*. Most of the constables chatted amiably to the marchers; the sergeant had nothing to say, except from time to time, "Keep in at the side, there's a car coming." The atmosphere was cheerful and good-humoured.

And then the nuclear power plant came into view. It sat right beside the sea, on a wide stretch of land protected by high fencing. The buildings shone white in the sunshine though even as they watched a cloud moved across the sun. The crowd was quiet now.

"Keep over!" trumpeted the sergeant. "If you don't keep right in to the side somebody'll get killed with all this traffic on the road. It's ridiculous bringing kids out on a thing like this."

Josie opened her mouth to make a retort then closed it

43

again. Emma raised her thumb to her. They moved in to the side.

Outside the plant gates were another half dozen constables, amongst them the woman who had spoken to Josie on the promenade. Josie remembered what the constable had said. *I'd be there with you* . . .

"We've got to remember that not all the police are bad," Emma had said at a meeting, "or against us." Emma was sensible. "You could do to model yourself on that nice Emma Hunter, Josephine," Aunt Gladys had said many a time, when they were younger, and it had been almost enough to put Josie off Emma. But she was glad it hadn't. She looked at her friend and saw that she was even paler than she had been when they started out, yet was still struggling valiantly along. "Are you all right, Em?" she asked. Emma nodded. "Fine," she said.

Josie and Phil led the crowd on to a large piece of waste ground opposite the site. It belonged to a local farmer and he had given them permission to use it.

While they were sorting themselves out, an occasional spot of rain touched their faces. Glancing anxiously at the sky, they saw that the clouds looked thick and dark. And then a bicycle came whizzing down the road heading towards them.

"It's Marge!" cried Emma.

Marge jumped off and threw down the bicycle. "Whew! I thought I was going to be too late."

"So you changed your mind," said Jack, giving her hug.

"How could I *not* come?"

The Press had also arrived, two men with cameras slung around their necks and two carrying notebooks. They came and stood on the edge of the crowd.

"Are you ready, Josie?" asked Jack.

As ready as she'd ever be, she said, and felt a little sick in the pit of her stomach. Jack and Phil quietened the crowd and Josie got up on a small hillock to address it. They looked up at her, expectantly. What could she say that they did not know already? And what a nerve she had to be making a speech to some of them who were twice and three times her age!

"Thank you for coming," she began and her mind went blank. Totally blank. Like a television screen from which the programme has been wiped. She could see the blank screen inside her head. And nothing else.

Seven

The sea of faces floated in front of her, blurring together. Surely to goodnes she wasn't going to faint! She had never fainted in her life and this didn't seem to be the right moment to make a start. A baby cried and his mother comforted him. She heard the mother's voice saying, "There, there, Andrew." She felt desperate. And then she caught the eye of Mr Greig and he nodded at her encouragingly. You can do it, he seemed to be saying.

"It's great to see so many of you out today," she went on, stumbling a little, "mums and dads and kids and grannies too! You know why we're here — " For a moment she couldn't think why they *were* there. *Was* there any point in being there? Steady, McCullough, pull yourself together! "We're here because we're worried about having a nuclear plant on our doorstep. We're here because we think we've got a right to have a say in our future. We're here because we're *worried* about our future." As she went on she warmed up, and before long was speaking fluently, and passionately. She was aware of the adrenalin flowing, and of a great energy in her body.

The cameramen snapped her in mid-speech. They photographed the crowd, too, and their banners and posters.

Josie spoke for ten minutes, finishing up, "We demand a new public enquiry. I urge you all to continue pressing for it in every way you can!"

They clapped and cheered.

"Well done!" Jack slapped her on the back.

"You were great," said Marge and Emma smiled and nodded. "Though don't be getting too swell-headed," Marge added and ducked sideways as Josie made to give her a playful punch.

The two reporters came forward to interview them. What did they plan to do next? they asked. Lobby their M.P., they answered, write to the newspapers and everybody they could think of, like the Prime Minister, the Minister for Energy and local councillors, and encourage others to write; take petitions round; get people to put posters in shops.

"And do you think it'll get you anywhere?"

"At the very least," said Josie, "it'll make people more aware of what is going on."

At half-past two, Rod happened to be passing again down the street where Frank Oswald traded in ironmongery. As he approached the shop he squeezed on his bicycle brakes and slowed himself right down. In the porch were Josie's uncle, in the act of unlocking the door, and beside him, the straight-backed figure of his wife. The very straightness of her back suggested she was quivering, like a tautly held knife blade. "She runs on indignation," Josie had once said. "It's fuel to her fire." Remembering her words, Rod smiled. And then he saw, coming from the other end of the street, Josie's mother, hurrying, a little pink in the face.

On looking round, her relatives spied her also, and waited. Rod reached the shop at the same time as Mrs McCullough.

"Ah, Rod!" She greeted him warmly, obviously pleased to have a diversion.

He put his foot down on the ground and said hello.

"Oh, hello, there, son," said Mrs Oswald. "Didn't see you for a minute there. Out for a run, are you? It's a good healthy thing to be doing on a Saturday afternoon. Unlike what some others are getting up to."

"You didn't go out on that damned demonstration then, lad?" said Mr Oswald. "Got too much sense, I'm sure."

Rod shifted uneasily, unwilling to be aligned with the UFO and his wife against Josie yet not knowing what to say. He shrugged, then said, "They think they're doing the right thing."

"*Right* thing!" snorted Mrs Oswald. "Marching along the street with banners. Like common riff-raff."

"I believe Mrs Hunter is there," said Mrs McCullough.

"She's a nice woman," said Mrs Oswald," but a bit misguided, if you ask me." And she gave Rod a meaningful look as if she expected him to agree.

"Well, there's nothing to get too steamed up about, Gladys," said Mrs McCullough. "All Josie is doing is walking along the road to the site, with police permission."

Josie and her friends did not, though, have permission to lie in the road. Twenty of them had decided to do it.

The demonstration had broken up, the crowd was dispersing, making its way, in more straggly fashion than it had come, back towards the town. The attention of the police was diverted.

"There's going to be an accident here, I can see that," said the sergeant and went striding off as a lorry lurched around the corner sending people scuttling into the side.

"Right?" said Jack.

"Take care!" said Emma.

"Bring us a nail file," said Josie.

The twenty went quickly across the road. Joining hands, they stretched out across the site entrance and lay down.

Immediately, the alarm was raised. A shout went up from a constable and the sergeant came lumbering back, his face purpling, with several other constables at his heels. And behind them came the lorry, its back heaped high with concrete blocks.

The sergeant raised his loud-hailer to his mouth. "I would

advise you all to clear the roadway." His voice boomed out over their heads. "This is private ground belonging to the Electricity Board and you are contravening a bye-law by trespassing. You are also causing obstruction and, for that, I must warn you, you could be charged."

They did not answer. They continued to lie on the ground. Marge lay close to Josie, their arms touching, their hands still clasped. Swivelling her eyes round, Josie saw that her friend was staring upward, at the cab of the lorry, which had come to a halt. Out of the cab window poked the head of Marge's father. He was staring down at his daughter as if he could not quite believe what he saw.

The sky at the back of the lorry was dark now, Josie noticed, very dark. She shivered, feeling suddenly chilled. Time seemed almost to have stood still. And it had gone strangely quiet. She thought of the people, often groups of women, who during the Highland Clearances in Scotland in the 18th and 19th centuries had stood in the roadway obstructing the path of the sheriffs' officers who carried writs of eviction.

And then the rain came, mild in the beginning but swelling soon to a torrent. They brought up their arms to shield their faces.

"Right, men!" Josie heard the sergeant cry above the sound of the rain. By now she thought she would recognise his voice in a crowded football stadium.

And so the constables came forward to remove them. The demonstrators did not resist — they had all been agreed about that — but neither did they help. They let themselves go limp, like dead weights. Some of the police were relatively gentle, others were not. Josie did not get a gentle one, had not expected to. Somehow or other, she felt she would be picked out. It was the sergeant himself who came for her.

As he pulled her by the shoulders along the ground he caught hold of her hair, perhaps by mistake, perhaps not, but he did not let go. She bit her lip hard. She would not scream, she *would not*. He saw her pain and she saw the look on his face. Serves you right, it said: you asked for it.

Within minutes, the twenty had been dragged across the road and laid out on the ground opposite. The police towered over them, defying them now to get to their feet. The sergeant released Josie's hair and the pain stopped. She closed her eyes for a moment with the relief, not even caring how wet she was.

Opening her eyes, she saw a circle of faces around them. Not all of them were crowned with police helmets. A number of people had come running back when they'd heard there was trouble.

"Are you all right?" Mr Greig called out.

"Keep back please, everyone!" shouted the sergeant. "Right back!"

Josie came up to a sitting position and hugged her knees to her chin. The rain was easing. Thank goodness for that at least. Her backbone felt as if a scraper had been taken to it. She should have had her anorak hood up and her hair tucked into it. She would know better next time.

"How're you doing?" she asked Marge.

"Getting dragged along the road was nothing compared to the look my dad gave me! I might be out in the street with you looking for digs."

"Almost two thousand," said Khalil, producing his calculator. He had decided to join them in the end, after a great deal of heart searching.

They stopped talking when they saw two police wagons approaching.

"Are you going to walk or do you want to be carried?" asked the sergeant.

No co-operation, that was what they had decided. The constables returned. The girls they picked up and carried into the wagon, the boys were dragged.

"It's like the Tokyo underground in here," said Josie. They could hardly move their arms in the crush inside the wagon.

Two constables got in at the back beside them, another two sat up front with the driver. Steam rose from their wet clothes and clouded the windows. They set off back towards the town.

In spite of not being needed in the shop, Mrs Oswald remained there for the afternoon, retreating into the back whenever a customer came in whom she did not wish to speak to. That meant anyone who might know that her niece was out on the demonstration.

"Not just out on it but leading it! That girl of yours has given me a right red face, I can tell you!" she said several times to Mrs McCullough, who was anxiously watching the street. Rod had been past again and when he had seen her at the door he had stopped to ask if she had any news of Josie. "I wouldn't worry," he'd said. "It takes a while to walk up there and back."

"Business is slow the day, right enough," said Mr Oswald, coming to join Mrs McCullough at the door. "Mind you, it's a wet afternoon."

"It'll be that march that's doing it," said his wife.

"That means that a lot of your customers must be out on it," said Mrs McCullough and turned away to hide her smile.

As the afternoon dragged by, with no sign of Josie, worry turned in her like a knife.

They drank several cups of dark brackish tea brewed by Mrs Oswald who, when she had nothing else to do, put the kettle on. She couldn't abide being idle. With her tea she consumed a number of slices of seed cake, her favourite cake, and as she chewed she sighed, audibly.

Now Mrs Oswald had a friend called Mrs Crabbe who was a gossip of the first degree, and pious with it. She carried her news — usually bad — from door to door, street corner to

51

street corner, shop to shop. "You'll never believe it!" was usually her opening cry.

And so, when Mrs McCullough glanced up and saw Mrs Crabbe on the other side of the glass door, her hand on the handle ready to turn it, she knew that she would be coming in, not to buy six inch nails or paraffin, but to relay the latest news, and that it would not be good.

Eight

There were five of them, all girls, in one cell. They sat on the floor with their backs against the walls. It was warm in the room, hot even; too hot, although they had welcomed the warmth at first. They had stripped off their sodden anoraks and damp sweaters and opened the necks of their shirts and rolled up their sleeves. They had been told to leave their shoes outside in the corridor. In one corner stood a bed, with a bare mattress and no blankets. The electric light bulb had no shade on it. There was no window.

"Cosy," said Josie.

They sang songs. Their possessions — watches, belts, jewellery, money, even packets of polo mints and bars of chocolate — had been taken from them. One of the girls, Trish, had asked for a drink when they were being put into the cell, as she had been feeling sick after the ride in the police wagon, and been given a cup of water. It had been brought by a policewoman, not the one that Josie knew, but another who had a blank face and said not a word. She had stood over Trish while she'd drunk and taken the cup away afterwards.

"So that we won't do ourselves an injury", said Marge cheerfully.

They felt cheerful. It was because they were together, they agreed. To be on one's own would be quite different. They presumed that the other five girls who had been arrested would also be together.

After some time had passed, the door opened and the policewoman called, "Margery Gibson! Bring all your clothing with you."

Marge got up.

"Good luck," whispered Josie softly and raised her thumb.

Marge followed the constable out and the door clanged shut and was relocked from the outside. The four left in the cell listened to their footsteps fading away along the corridor. Felicity bit her lip.

"You'll be all right, Flick," said Josie. "Don't worry. Just don't let them get under your skin." It was what the sergeant would try to do to her, she knew. He had it in for her, saw her as the ringleader. The troublemaker. "Keep cool, calm and collected. The three cs. That's what my mother always says."

At the thought of their mothers, the girls quietened a little.

"My mum'll be worried sick," said Felicity.

"So will mine," said Marilyn. "And she won't be too pleased either. Not that she's for the power station but she'll have a fit when she hears I've been arrested."

None of them regretted it though, they were all agreed about that. They had discussed it thoroughly beforehand, and considered the consequences of their action and their families' reactions. It was not something that mothers expected to happen to their daughters, Josie said: that was one of the things *her* mother had said to her. "It's not easy sitting at home, Josie, waiting for a call from the police station to tell you they've arrested your daughter."

The door opened again and the policewoman called, "Felicity Black!"

Felicity got up.

"*Courage*," said Josie in a strong French accent.

Felicity followed the woman and the door clanged shut and was once more relocked. Now there were three in the cell.

"Looks like Marge has been allowed to go," said Marilyn.

"It'll take hours for them to get through twenty of us," said Josie.

They wondered what time it was, they had quite lost track

of it. For a while they sat, not talking, or singing, half drugged by the heat.

Then the door opened and the policewoman called, "Marilyn Sharp!"

Marilyn went leaving Trish and Josie. They stretched their legs in the extra space.

"Two green bottles," sang Josie, knowing which one would be the last to fall.

Outside the police station, Marge and Felicity waited with three of the boys who had already been released and half a dozen of the other organisers who had not taken part in the final demonstration. They stood close together, stamping their feet to keep warm. The rain had stopped but the wind had freshened.

"How did you get on?" the ones who had not been arrested wanted to know.

"Not too bad," said Marge. "They just asked my particulars and then read out the charge of obstructing the public highway."

"So you *were* charged!"

The boys said they had been pushed into their cell and one had tripped and gone down hard on his knees and been kicked by a policeman. There appeared to be more than one interview room. Two of the boys had seen the sergeant, neither of the girls had.

"He's the one to watch," said Marge. "I bet he interviews Josie."

Emma and her mother arrived bringing hot tea and sandwiches and while they were drinking and eating another car pulled up and a man and woman, whom nobody knew, got out with two large thermoses of coffee.

"We thought you could probably do with a hot drink," said the woman. "You must have got soaked right through, poor things!"

In the course of the next hour a number of people came offering help and bringing food and drink. Amongst them were Mr Greig and two other teachers.

And then the door of the police station swung open to release Jack and Marilyn. A cheer was raised and Marge rushed forward to hug Jack. Behind them came a police constable.

"You'll all have to move along now," he said. "You're obstructing the pavement."

"It's a very wide pavement, Constable," said Mrs Hunter. "What objection can you have? We're not preventing anyone from getting through."

"I'm sorry, madam, but it's against the law to have more than six people gathered together in a public place without giving due notice in writing."

"But more than six people often gather together on the beach without giving notice."

Marge strangled a giggle.

"That's different," said the constable, easing his hat back off his forehead.

"How is it, Constable?" Mrs Hunter's Scottish accent was more marked than usual. "We're simply taking some refreshment, just as they do on the beach. And waiting for some friends."

"Some of them'll be a while. You'd be as well going home and waiting for them there. Now just move along, if you don't mind." He came down the steps, holding out his opened hands, palms towards them, to shoo them away.

They moved round the corner.

"Good for you, Mrs Hunter!" said Marge.

"I'm certainly not going to be bullied! They can arrest me as well if they've a mind to. More tea, anyone?" She looked up the street. "Is that not Josie's mother coming?"

Mrs McCullough was out of breath when she reached them.

"Any word of Josie?" she asked.

The door opened and the nice policewoman looked in. "Patricia Cooper?" To Josie she said, "Shouldn't be too long now." She took Trish out and relocked the door.

Josie stood up and stretched her arms above her head. She felt stiff and a bit headachy from the stuffiness of the room. She longed for a breath of fresh air and a long cool drink. Two or three hours must have passed, she supposed, perhaps four, or five, since they had been brought into the room. The last part, when she and Trish had been on their own, had seemed the longest. At one point they had thought they must have been forgotten, or that they were going to be left overnight. They had felt subdued. But the sight of the nice policewoman had cheered her.

She walked round the room and did some exercises to ease the stiffness out of her muscles. After that, she lay on the mattress, with her arms folded above her head. It seemed to have gone very quiet in the building; she could hear no sound of anything at all, not of voices nor of footsteps nor of traffic outside. She wondered how it would be to be locked up for days, or weeks.

She had dozed off into a light sleep when she heard the key being turned in the lock. Jerking upright, she saw the policewoman, the nice one, opening the door.

"How are you?"

"All right. A bit deyhdrated."

"I know. They should have given you a drink."

"Are you the only civilised one?"

"Some of the blokes are all right too."

"But not the sergeant?"

"No comment. Are you ready then?"

Josie put on her shoes and followed the constable. The door was not relocked this time. The cell was empty.

"Am I the last one?"

"I'm afraid so."

The constable led her into an interview room and said she should sit down. She herself remained standing, beside the door, looking straight ahead.

There was a clock on the wall. It said nine. Josie exclaimed aloud! She had had no idea that it was quite so late. Very soon, she told herself, I will go home and have a drink and a bath and go to bed and sleep the clock round. She did not want food; her appetite had long since gone.

After ten minutes had ticked by, the sergeant came in with two other male constables. He sat down behind the desk; they stood.

"Is this your bag?" asked the sergeant, picking up the canvas satchel that Josie had worn over her shoulder.

"Yes."

He turned it upside down and the contents tipped out and went scattering and rolling all over the floor. "Are these your possessions?"

"Yes."

"Better pick them up then."

One of the male constables snickered. Josie looked at the sergeant, he looked at her. If she did not get down and pick up her things they would lie there and probably be swept away in the morning.

She squatted down and picked up her purse, a notebook, a nail file, three used bus tickets, a paper tissue, two band-aids, an elastic band, a length of scarlet ribbon, and a comb. To retrieve two biros, an eyeliner pencil and the money that had spilled out of the purse, she had to crawl half under the table and push a waste paper basket out of the way. She felt the men's eyes resting on her, with amusement. She took a deep breath and counted to ten before she got back up and sat on the chair again.

The sergeant was holding up a screwdriver. "This yours too?" She acknowledged that it was. "What were you doing with a screwdriver in your bag?"

She shrugged and said she didn't see why she shouldn't have a screwdriver in her bag.

"It could be used as an offensive weapon. It's not usual to find a girl carrying a screwdriver around."

"How — ?" she began and stopped. She had been going to ask him how he knew what girls carried in their bags, but there seemed no point in getting off on that tack. And she had to be wary. For maybe the next thing he was going to suggest was that she had been carrying the screwdriver to use against the police. "My uncle has a hardware shop," she said, "and I work in it on Saturdays."

"So it just happened to fall into your bag?" The sergeant gave a little smirk and looked at one of the constables, the one who had snickered. His fan club, Josie presumed. She felt like snatching the screwdriver from his hand and plunging it into some soft bit of him, if any bit *was* soft. *Steady, McCullough, calm down!*

"My mother asked me to bring one home."

"I thought there would be plenty of screwdrivers in an ironmonger's house?"

"Not in our flat. We live on the top floor."

Or we used to live on the top floor, she might have added, for she doubted if they would be living there any more.

"Ask my uncle if you need to," she said, looking the sergeant straight in the eye.

He stared straight back at her for a few seconds then, lifting a piece of paper from his desk, said that he was going to read out the charge. But first, he asked her if she had anything to say and cautioned her that anything she did say would be taken in evidence and could be used against her.

"I have nothing to say," she said and waited. She feared he

might charge her with carrying an offensive weapon, which would be much more serious than obstruction. But he charged her simply with obstructing the public highway. She breathed an inner sigh of relief. She wondered whether he had had any intention of bringing the other charge. He might just have been trying to taunt her.

She was told she might go. The night air felt cool after the fuggy warmth of the police station. She paused on the top step to take a couple of deep breaths and to reorientate herself.

"Josie!" a voice called and in the next instant Marge had flung herself up the steps and was throwing her arms around her. "Your mum's round the corner."

When Mrs McCullough saw them coming she detached herself from the knot of people on the pavement and hurried to meet them. She and Josie embraced, without a word. Josie felt her mother's cheek wet against hers and for the first time since being arrested she shed tears herself.

Nine

"Well?" demanded Aunt Gladys, the moment Josie and her mother set foot in the hall.

"Well?" said Josie.

"Josie's tired, Gladys," said Mrs McCullough hurriedly. "Can we leave the post-mortem till the morning?"

"So Josie's tired, is she? Oh, I am sorry to hear that!"

"Look here!" said Josie, feeling less tired. "I'm not going to go through a whole song and dance act just so that you can tell me to get out of your house at the end of it — "

"Hold your horses, miss," said Uncle Frank. "We're prepared to give you a proper hearing. We're just and fair-minded people. Let it never be said of us that we are not."

"On you go into the sitting room," said Aunt Gladys, holding open the door.

"I'm not going anywhere. And I don't want a 'hearing'! I'm not going to be tried by you two. Who do you think you are — setting yourselves up as judges?"

"Don't you shout at us, Josephine McCullough," said Uncle Frank, coming towards her with his arm upraised.

"Go on, hit me! I dare you to! You'd live to regret it, that's all I can say."

"Stop it, both of you!" said Mrs McCullough, coming between them. She looked near to tears again and while Josie was sorry about that she was not going to back down before her bully boy of an uncle. He wouldn't have hit her though, she knew that, for his arms were wavering even as he was advancing towards her. He hadn't the nerve and he knew that she would have had him on the floor in a second. "This is terrible, brawling like this." Her mother's voice trembled.

"You're dead right it is," said Aunt Gladys, glaring at Josie. "The impudence of her!"

"Let's go to bed, Josie," said her mother.

"We'll settle this in the morning then," said Uncle Frank.

"We'll settle nothing," said Josie. "I'm not staying under your roof for another ten minutes. That's about all it'll take me to get my bag packed." She made for the stairs.

"And where do you think you're going to go at this time of night, madam?" said Aunt Gladys. "You can't walk the streets. Though maybe that's where you belong."

Josie looked back. "I'm going to stay with the Hunters. Dr and Mrs. They have already invited me. Knowing what you two are bloody well like!"

"How dare you — !"

Josie was already half way up the stairs, running, leaping over two and three steps at a time, leaving the angry voices behind. Her energy was back in no small measure and her blood on the boil. But she felt better now that she'd been able to release some of her aggro. She had bottled it up for so long that when she had lifted the lid it had gone off like a geyser.

She was packing a few things into her rucksack when her mother came into her room.

"Mum, I'm sorry, really I am — not about what I said to them, but for you."

"It's all right, love, I realise you couldn't put up with it any longer. I'll stay on for a few days until we find a place. I'll start looking on Monday."

"We'll get something, Mum. Even if it's only a room. And I'm going to try to find an evening job."

"But you've got your school work."

She would manage both, said Josie, as long as she didn't have her relatives to put up with as well. "Honestly, families!" She buckled her rucksack. "I'll ring you in the morning."

"We'll go and have lunch somewhere together. Take care!"

Josie kissed her mother and swinging her rucksack up on her back, she ran down the stairs.

Her aunt and uncle were still patrolling the hall.

"Just one moment, miss," said Uncle Frank, barring her passage. "We're not having you going round to the Hunters spreading lies about us."

"I'll spread what I like. But it won't be lies, I can tell you! Now would you mind getting out of my way." She gave him a little push and he rocked on his heels.

"Don't you dare put your hand on him!" said Aunt Gladys. "My, you've a queer nerve on you! No wonder you've landed in trouble. It's as well your father didn't live to see this day."

"Don't bring him into this," said Josie, her anger rising again. "How you ever came to be even his half-sister is beyond me!" She unbolted the front door and tugged it open.

"I'll have a word with Dr Hunter myself," said Uncle Frank.

"Have a word with whoever you like — I'm not worried."

She went out into the porch and slammed the door shut behind her. I'm free, she thought, looking up at the sky, which was speckled with stars; of *them*, at least.

She fetched her bicycle from the back shed and wheeled it out on to the road. Glancing up at the top storey of the house, she saw her mother's face framed in her lit window. She waved. She did not look at the windows on the ground floor.

The Hunters were still up. "Of course you can stay, dear," said Mrs Hunter at once. "You're most welcome. I had a feeling you might be needing a bed tonight."

When the rest of the family had gone to bed, Emma and Josie sat on at the kitchen table talking over the day's events.

"I wonder when you'll have to appear in court?" said Emma.

"Couple of months maybe, perhaps less. They have to serve the summons on us first."

"They might drop the charges.".

"I bet they don't. They'll be wanting to discourage us from trying any further action."

"I bumped into Rod, by the way," said Emma.

"Oh?" Josie raised one shoulder in a slight shrug.

"I think he'd have liked to have come down to the police station. But it was kind of difficult for him."

"I don't see why."

"Well, with him not being part of it."

"That's his fault then, isn't it?"

Josie and her mother had lunch in a pub down by the harbour.

"Take care of yourself then, love," said Mrs McCullough, when they got up to go.

"And you, too," said Josie.

They kissed and parted. Mrs McCullough was going back to write an ad for the newspaper, and one to put up in the dentist's waiting room, and she had to work out a scale of charges for her physiotherapy sessions. Suddenly, she said, there seemed to be so much to do and to think about, what with flat-hunting and setting up in business!

She hurried off. Josie returned to the Hunters' taking the suitcase of clothes which her mother had brought. There was no one at home; the Hunters had gone to visit relatives. Josie went up to her room and opened a history book — she had to write an essay on the rise of the trade union movement in Britain — but found that she kept looking out of the window at the garden, and at the field behind, and at the sea beyond that. She threw down the book and went out for a cycle run.

And on the way down to the sea she met Rod, who was also out for a run on his bike.

"I'm sorry," she said, holding out her hand.

"So am I," he said, taking it.

"I was hoping I'd see you."

"So was I."

They laughed. They cycled on, side by side, and Josie made a resolution, a silent one, that she was not going to quarrel with Rod ever again, well, not this afternoon, anyway.

It was a bright autumn day with a nip in the air. The sea sparkled beside them. They cycled a long way down the coast, more than twenty miles. Both felt in need of some decent exercise. Neither mentioned the word 'nuclear' once Josie had given an account of the previous day's happenings. Yes, we must just agree to differ there, she thought; Rod was right about that. Today, it seemed possible to do so. Today, she was glad to forget about yesterday, for a while.

They came to a town, one much like their own, with a small harbour now used more by yachtsmen than fishermen, and a promenade backed by hotels and houses advertising bed and breakfast. In a cafe overlooking the water they ordered fish and chips and a pot of tea. As they ate they watched the colour ebbing from sea and sky.

"I like living by the sea," said Josie.

"I'd like to live in the country proper," said Rod. "Do you know what I'd really like to do?"

"Tell me!"

"Have an Alpine garden. Run it as a nursery." He went on to talk enthusiastically about an Alpine nursery he'd visited in Inverness-shire.

"Sounds like you'd rather do that than engineering?"

"I think I might, you know."

They had to ride home in the dark. The sky had clouded over again; there was no moon, no stars either. Josie cycled behind Rod, keeping her eye on his rear light. Thoughts of her history essay intruded into her thoughts from time to time but not too insistently.

When they were within a couple of miles from home Rod

65

stopped and suggested going on to the beach. Leaving their bicycles, they went down through the dunes to the sea's edge. They watched the white waves come coiling out of the darkness. They felt the spray on their faces.

"It's quite warm," said Josie. "Well, not too cold."

"Almost warm enough to swim."

"Do you mean that? Are you game?"

"Are you?"

He scarcely had to ask.

"This is madness," said Josie, as they struggled out of their clothes in a sand dune. She laughed and ran ahead of Rod to the sea.

He went after her, just able to make out her dark outline. The waves washed over them making them shriek with agony and pleasure and sheer exhilaration. They waded through the waves and then plunging into the water they swam, parallel to the shore, though only for a few strokes, as the cold was biting and penetrating. Soon, they came galloping back through the waves to the shore.

"Keep moving!" said Rod. "Come on, one, two, three, four!"

They jumped up and down and did exercises and then they sprinted along the beach, stumbling now and then but regaining their balance immediately and carrying on. At the end of the strand they slowed.

"I'm boiling now," said Josie.

"Where are you?" asked Rod, catching hold of her hand and trying to draw her to him. But she stepped back, fully conscious for the first time of her nakedness, and of his.

"Rod, this could be dangerous —"

"I've never thought you were afraid of danger?"

"I just don't want us to get too heavy, not yet . . . I can't cope. I've got enough, more than enough . . ."

He said her name, that was all.

"I'm sorry, Rod." She was tempted to move towards him but knew that if she did the situation would go totally out of control. It was a commitment she couldn't take on board, for the present at least. She wanted to talk to him about it but how could they talk here, against the noise of the sea, and without being able to see the other's face? She was shivering, and the goosepimples on her upper arms felt like small gooseberries. "I'm sorry," she said again and began to run, back to where they'd left their clothes. Rod followed, staying a yard or so behind.

They went into the dune where they thought they had left their clothes but could find no trace of them. Searching with hands and feet, they floundered about in the soft sand amongst spiky clumps of whin. They must be in the next dune over, said Rod, but there too, they could feel nothing but sand and whin. They moved on to the next one.

"I'm sure this isn't it," said Rod, sending sand flying.

"Maybe someone's pinched them," said Josie and giggled and half-hicupped and giggled again. The ridiculous side of it had suddenly struck her. "Imagine — we might have to ride through the town *starkers*! Like Lady Godiva. We might even get arrested for streaking. 'But, Sergeant, I couldn't *find* my clothes.'"

"You'll have hysterics in a minute if you're not careful," said Rod, though it was beginning to get to him too.

"We might get into the *Gazette*. 'Respectable pillar-of-the-community ironmonger's niece seen cavorting naked with respectable pillar-of-the-community nuclear engineer's son.'"

They were both laughing and giggling now in the way that neither could remember doing for a long time, not since the times earlier in childhood when giggling comes on, sometimes for no particular reason, and cannot be controlled. Here, though, they did have a reason and every time they thought of it they went off into fresh convulsions.

But there came a point at which they could laugh no longer. Their stomachs ached and their sides ached and they were doubled right over.

"For dear sake!" said Josie. "At least I suppose while you're laughing you can't die of hypothermia."

"But where on earth are those damned things?" demanded Rod.

They gazed along the dark beach with its fine white edge of froth. They no longer had any idea where they might have left their clothes.

Ten

"We will have to look systematically," said Rod. "Start at one end of the beach and work along. They've *got* to be here."

Not necessarily, thought Josie, for she had known things disappear inside her own house and even though she had turned the place upside down she had never found them. Not to find their clothes on a long stretch of dark beach in the middle of the night seemed to her a distinct possibility. She saw herself crouching, unclothed, in the bushes of the Hunters' garden trying to attract Emma's attention. It must now be late, and the Hunters would be in bed, and she had no key.

Watching the grey blur that was Rod bobbing ahead of her as he went in and out of the dunes made her want to laugh again. But the cold was becoming too piercing to leave any energy for laughing. She hurried on, slipping and sliding. When they were back at the part of the beach which they had first searched, Rod gave a shout of triumph.

"I've found them! Look!" He held up a dark shape. "It's your anorak."

They scrambled into their clothes. There was sand everywhere, in every crease and fold, in their shoes, their hair, and even in their mouths. When they moved they felt the chafe of the tiny grains against their skin. But move they must, and as fast as they could. They stumbled back up through the dunes to where they'd left their bicycles, pausing for a moment to draw breath and empty their shoes again.

"I think I've got half the beach here," said Josie.

"Gosh, it's gone one," said Rod, squinting at his watch.

"Oh no! How am I going to get in without ringing the bell?" She could come home with him, he suggested, but she was worried that the Hunters would be worried if they didn't find her in her bed in the morning. She would get in somehow, climb in a window, or waken Emma. He was not to worry, nor come with her.

They cycled as far as the Hunters' corner together.

"Are you sure you'll be all right?" he asked.

"Certain. I'm a dab hand at climbing in windows. And I'm sure I left my bedroom one open."

"See you in the morning then," he said and kissed her. "Later in the morning!" He kissed her again.

"Go on!" she said and blew a kiss after him.

She ought to know when to keep her mouth shut, she thought, when she stood gazing up at her fully closed bedroom window. Talk about tempting Providence! She was good at that. She was good at everything that caused trouble. And inconvenience. It was certainly inconvenient to be locked out in the middle of the night and she wouldn't dare ring the bell. If she did, it would be sure to be Dr Hunter whom she disturbed. And he would be sure to have just got into his bed and fallen asleep after being called out on an emergency.

She would have to try the old gravel routine which she had read about but never put into practice. First of all, it seemed to be difficult to find the right kind of gravel. A handful of soil wouldn't even make the distance up to Emma's window. The path was paved. But she thought that the next door neighbours' drive might be gravelled.

After taking a good look up the road, she slipped along to the neighbours' gate, which, mercifully, was standing open. She went just inside it and, bending down, scooped up in her hands a heap of gravel. Half-bent over, gravel trickling from between her fingers, she shuffled back to the Hunters' house.

She positioned herself beneath Emma's window. Now! she

told herself and flung her arm up in a wide arc. Some of the gravel struck the window — she heard a faint rasping sound as it did. It would take a lot more than that to waken anybody! And Emma was a heavy sleeper.

Josie contemplated the situation. Should she go back for more gravel? It didn't seem worth it, especially since she would lose half of it again on the return journey. And what if the gravel-owners were to look out of their window and see her? See her *stealing* gravel? *Josephine Rona McCullough, did you on the night of* — ? There seemed to be no end to the charges she could be had up on.

"Emma!" she called up, with some desperation, and in a hoarse whisper. Her throat felt as if it were lined with grit. "Emma," she called again, more loudly.

A church clock struck two, the notes carrying clearly and resonantly on the night air. Where was she going to spend what was left of the night? She tried calling Emma once more before she gave up and went to look for alternatives.

The garage was the first place she thought of, since the back seat of the Hunters' station wagon would provide a reasonable bed. The door was locked. She tried the garage window but it, too, was immune to her tugging. She went round the back into the garden. There was a tool shed but it was full of lawnmowers and hedge clippers and hoes and spades, everything that was sharp and disagreeable. And then there was the greenhouse. She settled for that.

It was warm inside the glass house; the heating must be on. She spread an old potato sack on the floor and lay down. She slept.

"Goodness gracious, is that you, Josie?" said a voice, dragging her up from the very depths of her slumbers. She jerked upright and for a moment could not think where she was. She was aware of green leaves in profusion crowding above her and the glint of glass and then, as her eyes focussed, she saw Dr Hunter bending over her.

"I thought you were a tramp for a minute there," he said.

No doubt she looked like one. She ran her fingers through her hair and felt the sand squeak in it. Her back ached and she winced when she tried to straighten her legs.

"I got locked out."

"You should have rung the bell, silly girl! Away on in now and have a good hot bath and some breakfast."

The bath eased her back and the knots in her limbs; she could have lain in the warm silky water all morning.

When Rod saw the Hunters' door opening and Emma coming out with Josie he couldn't help feeling disappointed, even though he knew it was not very reasonable of him.

Josie walked in the middle between him and Emma and treated them to an amusing account of her time spent under glass. At the end of the next street they were joined by Marge and the conversation then turned to Marge's father.

"He can't see past his job, that's his trouble. He's accusing me of trying to do him out of it."

"Wait till you get your summons!" said Emma.

"That's when my mum'll do her nut and all. The idea of me up in court!"

"Or in prison," said Josie.

"You're not going to go to prison?" said Rod.

"We might. If we refuse to pay the fine. Though possibly they wouldn't send Marge since it's her first offence. Don't forget — I've already got a record! For holding a candle on the church steps."

"You're crazy!"

"It's a matter of principle. Of making a stand."

He was stunned. She had turned away to speak to Emma. Did she know what she was talking about when she glibly referred to going to prison as if it were no more than taking a walk down the road? He'd once seen a television documentary about women in Holloway. He'd been horrified.

The school came into sight and now they were hailed by Jack and Phil who tagged on and, shortly afterwards, by Khalil. The talk was all of Saturday's demonstration. The pavement was not wide enough for so many; Rod found himself walking in the gutter. He dropped back, and Josie stayed with him, leaving the others to move ahead.

"You're not *seriously* thinking of going to prison, are you?"

"Yes, I am *seriously* thinking. What other way could you think about prison?"

Josie was greeted by two girls, Trish and Felicity. Rod let them go on.

He found it difficult to concentrate in school that morning. He kept thinking about Josie in a locked room, in *Holloway*.

Josie did not mention prison to her mother — there would be time enough to do that if and when she decided to go. At the moment the search for somewhere to live was enough to be getting on with.

They met in the White Owl and when Josie went to the counter to get their coffee she asked the owner if he needed any help. Marge, who worked in his fish and chip shop, had suggested that she should.

"As a matter of fact, I could use some. Evenings, six to eleven, Monday to Friday. I've got other help on at week-ends."

"What would you pay?"

They discussed wages and came to an agreement.

"Start next Monday?"

Josie paused for a moment to consider and during that brief space of time visions of meetings and homework and Rod and flat-hunting flashed through her mind and it all seemed impossible. But she had to make it possible. Her mother wouldn't earn much for a while and her widow's pension didn't go far.

"Right, I'll take it!"

"Good." They shook hands on it over the counter. "Call me Gino, by the way," he said.

Josie went back to tell her mother who, as she expected, was not pleased.

"I'll manage, Mum. I've got to give it a go."

"Oh, all right! But if your school work starts to suffer then you must promise me you'll give it up."

Mrs McCullough had called in at an estate agency and been given the addresses of two possible flats, and had found another in a newsagent's window. "Shall we make a start?"

The first flat overlooked the promenade and had a sea view.

"I could only let you have it for six months," said the woman straight away. "I let to summer visitors the rest of the year."

"Six months would be all right," said Mrs McCullough.

The woman led the way up two flights of stairs. The arrangement was similar to that at the Oswalds'; they would have to go through the house to reach their flat.

"I keep the place spick and span, as you can see. I always say you could eat off my floors." She ushered them in to the flatlet which consisted of two rooms and a kitchenette in a cupboard. "Share the bathroom on the floor below. You can have two baths a week each, but not in the mornings. And I expect the bathroom to be left as clean as you find it." She looked at Josie. "And we don't like any comings and goings after ten-thirty."

In silence they examined the spick and span rooms, which were adequately furnished in slightly sickly shades of ochre yellow and beige-brown. The spick and span woman stood waiting for their verdict.

74

Mrs McCullough cleared her throat and said, "Very nice. We'll um — have to talk it over, of course."

They shouldn't take too long talking, said the woman; flats as good as hers got snapped up like hot cakes.

"No," said Josie, when they were outside the gate.

"I agree," said her mother.

The next flat on the list was not really one at all, being merely two rooms in a large house, with shared facilities, but it was in a nice part of town. And it was cheap, especially for that area.

"Rooms wouldn't be ideal," said Mrs McCullough, "but it might do in the meantime."

The house was large and detached and surrounded by a jungle of a garden. Fir trees and holly bushes pressed against the ground floor windows. Paint was peeling from the window frames and the steps leading up to the front door were breaking up.

"One understands the low rent," murmured Mrs McCullough, as they waited for the door to be opened.

A cheerful old man appeared on the top step. "Come in, ladies," he said, "come in!" He looked as if he would not worry what time Josie came in at night. They followed him into an uncarpeted hall and up an uncarpeted stair. There would certainly be no question of eating off the floors here. Wallpaper hung in strips from the walls. The house was let out, he told them, to a number of different tenants who shared the kitchen and the two bathrooms. When Mrs McCullough asked how many he seemed uncertain, but, on being pressed, said it might be eight.

"And with us that would be ten?"

"Something like that. But it's a big kitchen."

The rooms, which were on the attic floor, were not big. But then of course neither was the rent, as the man pointed out. The beds looked as if they might have bugs and the chairs as if they would collapse if sat upon. There wasn't much else in the rooms.

"There might be something bigger available soon."

"Is someone leaving?" asked Mrs McCullough.

"In a manner of speaking." He winked.

They then went to inspect the bathrooms. The fitments appeared to be the originals, from the Victorian era, which might have been picturesque if the porcelain on the baths had not been green with verdigris and the washbasins frazzled with cracks.

Mrs Spick-and-Span would have a fit, thought Josie, wrinkling her nose. She herself was not frenetically fussy about cleanliness but the idea of actually getting into one of the baths or putting her feet on the rotting linoleum made her flesh squirm. And as for the lavatories, they were unspeakable!

Two elderly men were cooking on the ancient gas cooker in the kitchen. One was half coughing up his lungs. Was he the tenant who might be departing soon? He spat into a greyish handkerchief and resumed frying an egg. The room smelt of cabbage and drains and cat. The McCulloughs escaped as fast as they could and made their way to the third and last address.

This flat had another pinched-nose woman reminiscent of Mrs Spick-and-Span to go with it but at least it was self-contained and had its own entrance round the side of the house. And the furnishings were fairly new and brightly coloured. Josie and her mother nodded to one another. They would just be able to afford the rent.

The woman, who had been eyeing Josie quizzically, said, "You're not Glad Oswald's niece, are you? The one that went out on that march?"

It turned out that she was a friend of Aunt Gladys's, so that was the end of that. The McCulloughs retreated to the pavement.

"What about a tent?" said Josie.

Eleven

"Recorded delivery for you, Josie," called Mrs Hunter from the front doorstep.

Josie went to sign for the letter. The envelope looked official and she knew at once what it would contain. There was a second letter for her, an unofficial looking one, bearing a Belfast postmark and addressed in the handwriting of her friend Rachel. She took both letters upstairs to her room.

She ripped open the official one first. She was summoned to appear in the county court on a day in November on a charge of obstruction. So it was really going to happen. Until now it had been something to talk about, something not quite real. She put the date in her diary and saw that it fell on the Monday following half-term. They had been discussing whether or not to pay the fines. Some, like Felicity and Marilyn, said they were being pressurized at home to pay; others, like Marge, were swithering. Jack and Phil thought they probably would not pay. As did Josie, though she had not quite decided. It might depend, too, on the state of health of her own mother. Khalil said he must pay, for his father's sake. "We cannot afford too much trouble."

Josie ringed the date in red and closed her diary.

Then she turned to her other letter. It was indeed from Rachel, her oldest friend. They had started school together when they were five. They'd been inseparable over the years. Rachel had covered several pages with scrawling green writing — she favoured green biros — bringing Josie up to date with all the news of their friends, and at the end she said, "Why don't you come over for half-term? I'd love to see you.

So would Brian." Brian was her brother and he and Josie had gone out together for a year.

Rereading the letter, Josie felt terrible pangs of home-sickness. She desperately wanted to see both Rachel and Brian again, and the streets of Belfast itself. But how could she afford to go? All the money she would earn at the White Owl would have to be saved towards rent for a flat.

The cafe was quiet between six and seven. This gave Gino the chance to introduce Josie to Mrs Mason, who worked in the kitchen, and show her where everything was, how to work the till and so forth. He was going to leave her on her own so that he could go on to one of his other businesses, the ice cream and chip shop where Marge worked two nights a week.

"O.K. now?" said Gino.

"O.K.," said Josie.

Before Gino left she asked if she could put up one of her anti-nuclear power posters. He considered for a moment, shrugged, pursed his lips and said no.

He spread out his hands. "Look, I don't want this thing any more than you do, but I have to think of my customers. Maybe some of them won't like to see that on the door and won't come in. I have many children to feed."

"You don't want them exposed to the risk of radioactive leaks though, do you?"

"All right, don't start on me!" He raised his hands in an attitude of surrender.

"Can I ask customers to sign the petition then? I'll keep it under the counter."

"Oh, very well. But watch who you ask eh?"

"Do you want to sign?"

"Later," he said and departed.

Josie served two women with coffee and chocolate biscuits. They were school cleaners, had just finished work. They sat by the window, with their shoes kicked off under the table, smoking and yawning. Were they potential signers? Josie wondered. There was only one way to find out.

"Oh, I'm not for it at all, love," said one. "After what happened in Russia? You must be joking."

"But this isn't Russia, Jean," said her friend. "They're not so bothered there, are they — I mean, about what happens to people?

"Oh, I wouldn't say that. They're human beings too, aren't they?"

Jean signed, her friend said she'd think about it. She didn't like to be rushed into anything. The two women went on arguing. Josie left them to it and went off to serve two men at another table who signed without any fuss. They were farm workers. They were worried about the effect on the crops. "Will anybody want to eat them?" they demanded. "You go to Cumbria! You talk to the farmers there about living next to Sellafield. You talk to fishermen about pollution in the Irish Sea. They say it's the most radioactive sea in the world, barring the Dead Sea."

Around eight, Phil came in, carrying his saxophone in a case. He'd been having a lesson. He ordered a coke and sat on one of the high stools at the counter to drink it. The others had gone petitioning, he said; he'd arranged to meet them here.

While he and Josie were talking, Rod arrived. He stood just inside the door for a moment looking at Phil and Josie then he nodded and went to take a stool at the other end of the counter. Annoyance spurted in Josie. Surely he wasn't going to start being jealous of Phil!

She moved along to serve him. "Why didn't you join Phil?" He shrugged.

"Oh, you'd drive me up the wall so you would!" She slapped his coffee down on the counter spilling it in the saucer.

"We're not special buddies."

"You used to be friendly enough."

The next arrival was Josie's mother who said hello to Rod and hello to Phil and settled herself in a table by the window. Josie went to her.

"I ordered a treatment table and ultra-sound machine today, love! I really feel as if I'm getting underway."

"That's great!"

"I don't know what we're going to do about a flat though. All the decent ones seem out of our reach."

"It might just have to be an indecent one."

"Yes, it might." Mrs McCullough smiled.

Between orders Josie managed to exchange a few words with her mother and throw the odd one in passing at Phil and Rod who continued to sit at either end of the counter, Rod reading a crumpled evening paper someone had left behind, Phil making notes on the back of an envelope.

And then the door swung open on a burst of talk and laughter and in trooped Marge and Emma and Jack and Khalil. They called out to Josie and headed for a corner table. Phil joined them.

They were in good spirits. They had done well with their petitioning and had sheets of paper covered with signatures to show for it.

"We must get everyone to write to the councillors and the M.P. too," said Jack. "We've got to keep the pressure up."

They were always talking about pressure, of two kinds, that which they must exert, and that which was being exerted on them.

"My father is getting nervous about me appearing in court," said Khalil. "The sergeant was in the shop this morning saying I'd better keep my nose clean in future."

"That's nothing but intimidation!" said Josie. "Picking on your father!"

Seeing Rod slide from his stool, she went quickly over to him.

"Are you off?"

"Well, you're too busy to talk, aren't you?"

"I can't help that."

"I never said you could. I was merely stating a fact."

She counted to ten inside her head.

"When will I see you?" he asked. "Apart from on the way to school — *running*?"

"You don't have to run with me."

"I want to. Will you keep Saturday night free anyway?"

She hesitated. The crowd was talking about going to a disco and she had half said she would go with them. She wanted to go. And Rod could come too. But she knew that he wouldn't.

"All right," she said.

"Pick you up at seven?"

She nodded. As he moved to go she said, "I do *want* to see you too."

"That's good." He smiled for the first time since he'd come into the cafe.

"I'll walk part of the way with you, Rod," said Mrs McCullough, getting up. They left together.

Josie chatted on and off to her friends until they departed shortly after ten. From then on most of the customers were men who'd been in the pubs and wanted a cup of coffee before going home. Josie collected more signatures, had the page almost full. Twenty-eight, she counted; room for only two more. Not bad, she considered, and at least she had achieved something.

Just as they were about to close, two men came in.

"Come on, dear, you can serve us. We've got to sober up before we go home and face the music." They seemed to find the prospect amusing and Josie wondered how their wives put up with them. "Two cups of black coffee and make it strong."

"Oh, all right!"

They drank it at the counter. She put the petition in front of them.

"Would you like to sign this?" she asked.

They hunched forward to read it. One of the men laughed, the other picked it up.

"Know what I think of your petition?" he said and slowly, holding the piece of paper well out of her reach, he ripped it in two, right down the middle.

Twelve

Josie raged all the way back to the Hunters'. She wondered
that there were not sparks flying off her. She wondered that
she did not look like a sparkler. On a bicycle. At least the
vision made her smile. She hadn't felt like smiling when the
man had ripped her petition in two.

The men had turned out to be employees at the power
station. They had no time for her, and 'her lot', and they had
told her so, in strong language. Bunch of nutters . . . should be
bloody well locked up . . . made to do National Service . . .

"Afraid of your own shadows. Make me want to pewk!"

Josie had tried to collect herself together and talk to them
rationally, but had not succeeded. After a couple of exchanges
she lost her temper and told them that they hadn't the brains
to think further than their week's pay packet and that as long
as they had their wages the rest of the population could go to
hell.

They were still arguing when Gino arrived to lock up.

"Didn't know you had a nuke nut working for you, Gino."
The man dropped the torn petition into the waste paper
basket. "Are you right, Billy?" he said to his mate and to Josie,
as he moved towards the door, "You want to mind your own
business." He looked back. "Otherwise — you might just
regret it."

"That sounds like a threat," she shouted after him. "*And*
I've got a witness!"

The men laughed and banged the door shut behind them.

"Now, look, Josie — " began Gino.

"They'd been drinking." Josie plunged her hands into the

waste paper basket and brought up the two halves of the petition stained with ice cream and orange juice. She smoothed them out. They looked like something the dog might have brought in but, sellotaped together, and ironed, they would be included with the other signatures. She was certainly not going to let those two jerks stop her!

"I told you," said Gino. "I want no trouble in here. The customer is always right, do you understand? If this happens again, then I have to ask you to go."

The following evening, the cafe was quieter, in the beginning.

For a while there were no customers at all and Josie managed to do a little French, though not much, for she found it difficult to concentrate. So many other thoughts kept pressing against the edges of her mind — her mother, flats, Rod, their court case, and Belfast, too. It was raining outside, heavy, bouncing rain which drummed on the pavement and flailed the window. Mrs Mason leant on the counter on the other side of the hatch with her head poking through, smoking a cigarette, watching Josie, making the odd comment, about the weather, and about having to cook hamburgers for a living, and about her corns which were playing up.

Shortly after the rain slackened, Mrs McCullough arrived. She put her umbrella to drip by the door, hung up her raincoat. There was something wrong, Josie knew at once.

"What is it?" she asked.

"It's just Aunt Gladys! We had a full-scale row this afternoon and I walked out."

"So where are you staying now?"

"I'm in a Bed-and-Breakfast further along the promenade."

Josie said she could come to the Hunters' but her mother ruled the idea out straight away. "I wouldn't be happy doing that."

Josie had to go and serve a customer. She called through to

Mrs Mason to make her mother a cup of coffee and a bacon roll. When she returned she said, "Now eat your roll! You want to grow up to be big and strong, don't you?"

Her mother smiled and did as she was told. "If only we could find a flat! We'll have to hope there's something in the *Gazette* on Friday." She hesitated then said, "I suppose you'll be busy on Saturday?"

"Why?"

"I'd love to go and see a film, maybe even have a bite to eat. But I expect you'll be seeing Rod?"

Now Josie hesitated. But when she thought of her mother sitting alone in a bed-sit she knew there was no choice. "I can see Rod any time. We'll go out and have a good time together, the two of us. I'll have my week's wages!"

"Are you sure, love?"

"Sure I'm sure."

Her mother's face had brightened and she went off looking cheerful.

Rod looked cheerful, too, when he came in. He was pleased to find that the cafe was quiet and Josie not so run off her feet that she could find time to stand and chat for a few minutes.

"Rod — about Saturday," she began.

"Don't tell me — !"

"I've got to go out with my mother. I *must*. She's having a hell of a time."

"So am I."

"Oh, don't be so damned stupid! You don't know what you're talking about."

Now she was angry with him. What did he know about bad times? His life was easy: he had a comfortable home, plenty of money, understanding parents, *two* parents . . .

After he'd gone and she'd simmered down, she admitted to herself that she hadn't been entirely fair. It wasn't his fault that his father hadn't died in a petrol bomb fire and that he had a room of his own and no need to work to earn money. But, on the other hand, she did think he was a bit selfish even objecting to her putting her mother before him. She sighed, said through the hatch, "I could be doing with a cup of coffee myself, Mrs Mason." While Mrs Mason was passing out the coffee the door of the cafe burst open as if propelled by an enormous gust of wind and a number of youths came surging in, pushing and shoving, kicking aside chairs which stood in their way, overturning one and laughing and then overturning another.

"Oh no!" said Mrs Mason. "Not that lot!"

One boy came up to the counter and leant on it. He looked about fourteen or fifteen. "Six cokes, fish face," he said and Josie smelt the beer on his breath. She was tempted to take the flat of her hand and push his face right back until he toppled over. However, she didn't fancy being flattened by his five mates.

"I don't serve anyone who speaks to me like that."

"Get that — she doesn't serve anyone *who speaks like that*!" He tried to mimic her voice. "Where are you from, Paddy?"

Lowering her arm, keeping her eyes on him, Josie lifted an empty lemonade bottle from the floor and set it on a ledge just below the counter top.

He leant further over until his face was only two or three inches from hers. "I *said* six cokes."

"And I said I wasn't going to serve you."

"You don't say so! Maybe we'll just need to give the place a bit of a doing over then, lads."

Whirling round like a dervish, he lifted a chair high above his head. Josie moved back against the wall and in the ensuing moment of silence she heard Mrs Mason suck in her breath. Then he crashed the chair down on to the floor breaking its back and knocking off a leg which went flying sideways narrowly missing the only other customer in the cafe, an elderly man, who ducked underneath his table. After that, as Mrs Mason said later to the police, all hell let loose.

Josie managed to snatch the telephone from the counter and dial 999. Mrs Mason snapped down the hatch and disappeared from sight.

They heard the wail of the siren within the next five minutes and then blue lights were flashing outside and there were police cars in the street and the youths were falling all over one another trying to climb over the debris and get out. They went straight into the arms of the police and collapsed, like pricked balloons.

All but the boy who had started the fracas. He took a running leap, placed one hand on the counter and vaulted over the top. Josie put out her foot and he went sprawling face downwards on the floor. Mrs Mason opened up the hatch and stuck her head through.

"Told you I'd done self-defence, didn't I?" said Josie.

"Just as well if you ask me." Mrs Mason gazed round the cafe. "You'd think a bomb had struck the place. Gino'll not be pleased to see this."

A constable came to collect the fallen youth who glared at Josie and looked as if he were about to spit when the policeman jerked his head round and led him away. Josie went to the door to see them off. Her mother wouldn't be pleased to hear about this either, would probably want her to give up the job. How is it, she'd say, things always seem to happen when you're around, Josie?

"Are you all right?" It was her friendly woman constable.

"Fine," said Josie.

"Some bunch they are," said Mrs Mason, coming to join them. "Drunk. Or on drugs. One or the other. I don't know what the world's coming to. I'm glad I'm not young."

"There's good and bad everywhere," said the woman

constable cheerfully. She took Josie's arm.

"Come on and we'll get you a cup of tea."

The station sergeant arrived while they were drinking it, the three of them sitting at a table surrounded by splintered chairs and upturned tables.

"Oh, it's you, is it?" he said, as soon as he saw Josie. "The nuke girl."

"She wasn't involved, Sergeant," said the constable quickly.

"*I* called the police," said Josie.

"So there's times when you think we can be helpful, do you?"

"Never said there weren't."

The constable was gazing down at her cup and rubbing her finger up the side of her nose. Careful, she seemed to be saying. Josie took her advice and said no more. There had been enough trouble for one night.

Josie had a good time with her mother on Saturday and on Sunday she went out petitioning with Marge after she'd finished at the kennels. They took their bicycles since they were to canvas an area on the outskirts of the town which bordered the coast. Most of the houses were expensive and sat in high, commanding positions overlooking the sea. Most of the owners would not sign.

"No, thank you," said one woman, half closing the door on them as if they were selling toothbrushes or sprigs of heather.

"But just think of the damage that Chernobyl has done," said Josie. "And it's not finished yet. Thousands could die of cancer over the next fifty years."

"If you'll excuse me," said the woman and shut the door right up.

"Stupid git," said Josie. "Money won't protect her from radiation."

The next house was even bigger, Victorian, with turrets and

virginia creeper covering its walls. The owner, an elderly widow who lived alone, invited them in to the drawing room and gave them tea which she served from a silver teapot, and offered them plum cake from a silver salver. They had a long chat. She was very concerned about the Laplanders, this woman, now that their reindeer herds had been contaminated and their livelihood wiped out by the fall-out from Chernobyl. She had spent much time when she was younger in the Arctic circle and had made a study of the Lapps.

She signed the petition. "Wholeheartedly," she said. "Do come back and see me again." And she insisted on giving them a donation of twenty pounds, towards expenses.

"That's fantastic of you," said Marge. "Thanks a million."

They would be back, they promised.

Their last port of call was a caravan park. Most of the vans were standing empty, and would remain so for the winter, but some were inhabited throughout the year.

"Of course!" cried Josie, as they cycled in through the gates. "Why didn't I think of it before? A caravan!"

Thirteen

"A caravan?" said Mrs McCullough. They were sitting in her bed-sit which looked out on to a small backyard cluttered with dustbins and discarded boxes.

"It's got a sea view," said Josie. "And it's as big as this."

"But there'd be two of us in it."

"There's a family of four living in one."

"Oh, all right, let's go and take a look."

Daylight was waning. The walk to the caravan park took half an hour. For the last part of the way, where there was no pavement, they had to dodge in to the side whenever they saw car lights approaching.

"Not terribly convenient, is it?" said Mrs McCullough. "Especially in the dark."

"You could get a bike. You used to cycle."

"But I haven't for ages."

"You could take it up again."

The park looked rather forlorn in the darkness, with only a few lights brightening it here and there. Josie cursed herself for not having waited until the next day so that she could have brought her mother to see it in daylight, but, as usual, once she had an idea in her head, she hadn't been able to wait.

The owner lived in a new bungalow at the entrance. Josie had already spoken to him. He passed over keys to three different caravans — or mobile homes, as he referred to them — and said they should take their time. "There's no hurry."

"I shouldn't think there was," said Mrs McCullough as they came out of his overheated bungalow to face the stiff breeze that was blowing in from the sea.

Josie linked arms with her mother. "Come on, let's go and see some dreamy mobile homes!"

The first one was right beside the family of four. The blare of their television set and the screaming of a young child could be heard from some distance off.

"This might not be the best location," said Mrs McCullough.

They passed it by and went on to the next van, which was sited in the far corner of the park. All the vans in this area were dark and silent.

"Listen to the sea!" said Josie.

They stood still and listened and heard the roar and swoosh of the waves as they struck the rocks below. The park was sited on a headland which jutted out into the water.

"Mm," said Mrs McCullough, shivering a little. She liked the sound of the sea but she was not sure how she would feel sitting up here alone on dark evenings listening to it and the moan of the wind. "After all, you would be out most evenings, Josie."

Josie was already opening up the door and switching on the light. They went inside and her mother admitted straight away that it was more spacious than she had expected. It had been well thought out and designed, with a place for everything.

"It's far nicer than that bed-sit," said Josie. "Cleaner and brighter. Look — fridge, cooker, wardrobe, loo — "

"Everything the modern home needs!" said Mrs McCullough. She was not too enthusiastic about the chemical toilet but agreed that beggars couldn't be choosers and she would not turn it down for that reason alone. "It feels so isolated though, dear." She stared out of the open door into the black night.

"Let's see where the other one is," suggested Josie.

It was situated nearer the entrance gate, which appealed less to her, but more to her mother, who, from there, could see the lights of the owner's bungalow. And there was another occupied van two doors along. An elderly couple lived in it, said Josie; they were retired fairground people who couldn't stomach the idea of living in a proper house. Her mother, though, she knew, could stomach the idea of living in one quite easily.

Mrs McCullough sat down to think it over. Josie forced herself to say nothing more. She *wanted* to come and live here, not just because they had to find a place of their own but because she liked the idea of living in a caravan. She liked the idea of limiting her possessions to the bare minimum. That way, there was less to bother about. That way, you felt that at any time you could set off, take to the road, travel the world.

"How much did you say it was?" asked her mother.

Josie told her. "We'd have to agree to take it for six months though, to get it at that price."

"That would be right over the winter. Oh well, let's take it! We've got nothing to lose."

There were advantages in having nothing to lose, Josie reflected, as she lay in her bunk right under the window on the night that they moved in. She had the curtain drawn back so that she could see the stars and the little golden slice of moon and when she listened she heard the hiss of the waves. It pleased her to be so close to the outside world. She did not envy her friends their more solid houses.

In the morning, on waking, she rose at once, washed and dressed and went out. The freshness of the air was exhilarating. She walked round to the back of the van and saw that from there they had a view right up the coast. It was the first time she had had a chance to look around in daylight. And she saw that they had a good clear view of the nuclear power station.

"With a pair of binoculars I'll be able to watch them at work."

"You'll be able to watch my dad," said Marge. "We had yet another row last night. He'd heard I was out petitioning. He says I've got to give it up or get out."

"You can have the spare bed in our house," said Emma.

"Thanks, Em, but I couldn't stay with you for long, could I? No, I just couldn't. I wish I could live in a caravan like you, Josie, but I'd need to have a full-time job before I could afford that."

"Leave school?" said Josie.

"It might come to that."

And it did. After another row with her father Marge walked out. She went to the Hunters' and two days later got a job on a till in a supermarket. "It won't exactly make me a fortune but I'll be able to survive on the wage."

"What about your A levels?" everyone asked. But she wasn't going to give up on that front, she said; she would study in the evenings. She gave up the chip shop, which she didn't mind at all, and the kennels, which she did. Josie took her to see Mr Walker, the caravan owner, and they negotiated for her to rent the van next to the McCulloughs at a reduced rate. "There's only one of her," said Josie, "and she's small."

"Oh, all right! You'd talk anyone into anything, Josie!"

So Marge started work and moved into the park. She and Josie cycled into town together in the mornings and, sometimes, when Josie returned from the cafe at night and saw that Marge's light was still on she would tap on the door and go in for a quick chat. Working the till at the supermarket was stultifyingly boring, said Marge, but in the meantime it suited her well enough, since it was not mentally demanding. The moment she left the store she could put it behind her and have her mind free for chemistry and biology. On Sundays, she came into the McCulloughs' van for breakfast. Sunday was their favourite day.

It was the day, too, that Mrs Gibson visited her daughter. She arrived with clean clothes and linen and enough food to feed Marge for half the week. Mr Gibson slept on Sunday afternoons.

On a Sunday afternoon when Jack had come to see Marge and Mrs Gibson had popped in to have a cup of tea and a chat with Mrs McCullough, Josie slipped out of the caravan and went down on to the rocks. Spume was flying high; she had to stay well back to avoid getting drenched. She needed a little space in the week when she didn't have to be rushing from one place to the next, when she could take time to think.

There were three things to think about.

One was their court case which was never far from their minds now that the date was coming steadily closer. Three weeks to go! At breakfast, only that morning, her mother had said, "I hope you're going to pay your fine and not go to prison?" She and Marge had both said they were still thinking about it. But Marge had to consider her job.

The second thing that Josie was thinking about was whether or not to go to Belfast for half-term. When she had written back to Rachel to say that she couldn't afford to come, her friend had responded by sending a return ticket. 'Now you have no excuse!' Had she been looking for one? Josie realised that she might have been since, with the ticket in front of her, she was still not sure whether she wanted to go. It would mean opening up old wounds, wounds which were not even half closed. One wound, in particular, and it was not all that old.

Her father was much in her mind these days; she kept imagining what he would say in different situations. What he would say about her her going to prison. "Wait," he used to say, "don't do anything until you know exactly what it is you want to do." And so she was waiting.

And the other matter that was occupying her thoughts was

Rod. They had not made up since the night she had raged at him in the cafe about being insensitive and not understanding the stresses in other people's lives. She knew she had gone over the top and she knew, too, that she wasn't much good at saying sorry, at admitting she was wrong. When they saw one another in school they nodded in passing, as if to say, "I see you there", but they kept their distance. She did not know what to *think* about Rod but when she did see him she felt the colour mounting into her face and her pulse rate increasing.

And so, when she looked up and saw him coming round the edge of the rocks, the same thing happened. It was as if by thinking about him she had called him up. But he was real enough. She saw the sandy-red of his hair against the grey rocks and the way he hunched his shoulders when he saw her and stopped. He looked so familiar, just even in the way that he stood, and held his head. For a moment neither of them moved. The gulls wheeled overhead with their raucous cries and the sea went on pounding against the rocks.

Then, slowly, Rod put a foot up on to the rock in front of him and began to move towards her. She got up and, taking her time also, went to meet him. This is crazy, she thought, even as she was going; it would be better if we were to leave one another alone.

He gave her his hand and she took it and they crossed the rocks to drop down on to the sand on the other side. Then, still without a word, he put his arm around her waist and they walked off along the beach.

Fourteen

Josie went to Belfast for half-term. She travelled by train to Liverpool where she caught the boat to Belfast. The sights, sounds and smell of the docks excited her and she was glad now to be going.

For the first part of the journey she stayed on deck, thinking, as she watched the English shore gradually recede, about their campaign. They had sent in the petitions containing some twenty thousand signatures, written to everyone they could think of who might be influenced, badgered shops to take posters, talked to people in the streets, and in a week's time would appear in court on charges of obstruction. Would it all make any difference? Will *they* pay any attention? *They* always seem to do what they want to do, to ignore the wishes of the people, except at election time. The only thing that worried most M.Ps., said Mr Greig, was the possibility of losing their seats. But their M.P. did appear to be listening. He had written to say he was pressing hard for another public enquiry. "It is obvious to me that public opinion *has* shifted," he said, when they went to see him at his surgery on a Saturday morning.

But would it be obvious to the Prime Minister and the government?

Rod said he would hate to be an M.P. But then he liked a quieter, more private life than Josie, so he said. "I like to be quiet and private too at times," she had retorted. She was being quiet and private now, on this ship, cutting through the slightly choppy waters of the Irish Sea.

Her relationship with Rod had been proceeding relatively

calmly since that Sunday when they'd made up again. Their meetings had been confined to occasional walks on the beach or cycle rides out into the country. He had given up coming into the cafe. Trying to talk there was too difficult, especially when any of her crowd was in. *Her* crowd, as he called them. Not his. But they had not had a single row since that Sunday!

A light drizzle was falling, reducing visibility. The English coast had disappeared, and with its going, Josie allowed her thoughts to shift from her new life there back to her old one, and to her destination.

Some soldiers passed her on the deck, their boots clattering, their voices making her lift her head and look round. There were a number of soldiers on the boat, bringing back to her the realisation that things were different where she was going. In the past four months she had got used to living without having to think about bombs or not going into certain places. The first reminder had come with the tight security they had had to pass through before getting on the boat.

For a few hours she went below and curling up in a corner of the lounge, she read, and then went back on to the deck so that she would not miss the first sight of the Irish coast.

It was already there, a faint glimmer on the horizon. She felt excited again. She could hardly wait for the boat to steam up Belfast Lough. She felt as if she were going home!

Rachel and Brian were waiting for her. She flung her arms round them both and they hugged one another in a tight knot, talking twenty to the dozen and laughing.

"It's great to see you, Josie!"

"It's great to be back."

They had brought their father's car to meet her. Brian drove and Josie sat in the front seat beside him, with Rachel leaning forward from the seat behind, keeping a hand on Josie's shoulder.

Just after they crossed Albert Bridge they had to stop to let a parade go by. An Orange parade. Josie watched with interest the passing of the fifes and drums, the men in dark suits with their bowler hats and orange collarettes stepping out in time to the music, the banner at the front rippling in the wind. NO SURRENDER, it said. The younger men in the march were hatless and walked with a jauntier, more aggressive step. She hummed the tune under her breath. *It was old but it was beautiful and its colours they were fine* . . . It was a tune that set the feet a-tapping. Unless, of course, you were a Catholic.

The parade passed; they drove on. Josie, seeing the city with new eyes, noticed the police stations grilled and barricaded, like forts, where once she would have taken it for granted; noticed, too, a Catholic church ringed with barbed wire for protection. They were travelling through Protestant East Belfast.

"The world's in tatty shape, isn't it?" she said. "There's a heck of a lot needs doing."

Rachel and Brian burst out laughing.

"Still the same old Josie," said Brian.

"What have you been up to over there?" asked Rachel. "I'm dying to hear all your news. Life's been dead dull since you went away."

Their parents gave Josie a warm welcome. "Sure it's marvellous to see you, girl," said Mr Magee. "Now, come on and sit down and take something to eat," said Mrs Magee. "I've got ham and eggs for you and potato bread — I know you're fond of that."

"Fantastic," said Josie. But could she first use the phone to send a message to her mother?

"On you go. I expect she'll be sitting there wondering if you got here or not, if I know Rona. I'm the same myself."

Josie went into the hall and closed the door behind her. She dialled and quite quickly, as if he had been waiting at the other end, Rod answered. "So you've arrived safely!"

"I've not come into the Lebanon, you know!"

"Were your friends there to meet you?" There was a slight edge to his voice. He knew that Brian was an old boyfriend.

"They were. I'll need to go now so as I don't run up their phone bill."

"Can I ring you during the week?" When she didn't answer he said, "Josie, are you there?"

"I'm here, Rod. But I'd rather you didn't ring if you don't mind."

"It isn't that you don't want him to know about me, is it?"

"No, it isn't. I'll probably tell him. I just want to be left in peace for a few days."

So she had put it badly and he was annoyed! She was tired, she said, she'd been travelling all day, hadn't had much sleep the night before. They finished without a row but not as warmly as they had parted the previous morning.

"Oh, honestly!" said Josie aloud, putting down the receiver.

The Magees were sitting at the table waiting for her. She found a second wind and her tiredness slipped away as, too, did thoughts of Rod.

Next morning, Josie took a bus and went out to the cemetery at Dundonald to visit her father's grave. Rachel had offered to come with her but she had wanted to be on her own. Brian had said he would pick her up afterwards.

In the shop beside the cemetery gates Josie bought a pot of chrysanthemums. She found the smell of massed blossoms suffocating and almost unbearable and she had to ask the man who was serving to be quick. "I'm in a hurry!" The thick, cloying scent had brought sharply back memories of that same smell which had invaded their house on the day of her father's funeral. Wreaths had been heaped high on his coffin; he had been well regarded and much loved.

She carried the chrysanthemums in front of her into the cemetery. They were bronze coloured and sturdy, suitable blooms for her father. She pressed them against her face as she walked up through the rows of graves, past the big old tombstones, in black and white marble and in granite, bearing the names of people who had died long since and must surely be forgotten. Her father's grave, being newer, was at the back of the cemetery.

For a few minutes she thought she could not find it and almost panicked. She had gone down the row which she considered to be the right one and seen no sign of it. She ran back and down the next row. There was no stone on his grave, it was too soon to erect one, for the ground must be allowed to settle first, but they had put a stone pot at its head with his name on it. DAVID MCCULLOUGH, it would say, in bold black letters. She could not see them. As she ran, the graves blurred before her eyes running into one another and the flowers bounced against her chest and some petals fluttered down.

"Calm down now, Josie McCullough," she told herself and, taking a deep breath, she slowed.

She found the grave shortly afterwards. It had been tidied but it was bare and flowerless. Squatting down, she placed the pot of chrysanthemums on the soil, pushing it in a little, making sure that it would not blow over in a puff of wind. Then she looked at the stone pot and her father's name standing out on it so bold and black and the tears came.

She allowed them to come. It was better to cry, she knew that, had known it from the first day. For the first few weeks after he died she had cried every morning on waking; each day she had had to face the fact again that he was dead. Sometimes, she had tried not to waken, to hold on to her dreams. Once, she dreamt that he was not dead, that it was all a mistake, and had wakened, joyful, ready to run through to

100

her mother and tell her the good news. And then, as she was throwing back the bedclothes, she realised that she had been dreaming.

"It's not fair," she said fiercely, aloud, when she had dried her eyes and scrubbed her face with her handkerchief.

Life is not fair: that is what he would say; and you cannot expect it to be.

If only he had not had to get so involved in controversial affairs, her mother had said after his death, he might have still been alive. Josie touched the chrysanthemum petals. One might as well say if only he had been like Uncle Frank Oswald going to his hardware shop every day and keeping 'a clean nose' . . . Her father had not been Frank Oswald, he had been David McCullough. And she was glad of that. "You only get one crack at life," he had said to her once. "So live it!"

She kissed her fingers and placed them briefly over his name, then she got up and walked back down through the cemetery to the gate.

Brian was waiting. He put his arm round her and squeezed her shoulders and asked if she was all right? She nodded.

"You're a brave one. You're your father's daughter, I fancy."

She loved him for saying that! She turned her head and kissed his cheek and he squeezed her again.

"What about a spot of lunch? I know a good place down at Strangford."

"That'd be lovely."

She felt happy and relaxed with Brian. They had a good lunch together, talking non-stop, remembering old times, and laughing too, and afterwards, when they went for a walk along the shore of Strangford Lough and he stopped to kiss her, she responded warmly. The Magee family was part of her life.

"I'm still very fond of you, Josie, do you know that?"

"I'm fond of you too."

They might have stayed by the lough all afternoon but for the thought of Rachel waiting at home. She was mad enough as it was, said Brian, that he had taken Josie off for lunch.

"We've only got a week, for dear sake!" said Rachel, when they returned. "How are Josie and I to get enough time to catch up?" She took Josie's hand and pulled her upstairs and into her bedroom. "Now I want to know *everything*!"

They sat on Rachel's bed, and Josie told Rachel about Emma and Marge and their campaign against the nuclear power station.

"Will you go to prison, do you think?"

"Possibly, if we were found guilty, and we're bound to be."

"That doesn't surprise me, knowing you — "

No one knows me all that well, thought Josie, although they all think that they do; not what I am really like inside. Even Rachel, who had known her all her life, thought that if she went to prison it would be because she was a daredevil and didn't like to say no to a challenge.

"Rachel," she said, "apart from thinking it would be right to go, I'd quite like to have the experience. I suppose you think I'm daft?"

"I think you're an eejit!"

"But I want to find out what it's like for all those women who get put away. I want to see for myself."

"But think of being locked up!"

"I could cope, I think. I feel strong enough inside myself." Though who could tell what it would actually be like once she was inside without the choice of coming out?

"Any boys on the scene?" asked Rachel, changing the subject, and when Josie shrugged and half smiled, said, "Come clean!"

Well, said Josie, there was one boy called Rod but they were just good friends. "Oh yes?" said Rachel. But there was no time for her to ask any more questions as the doorbell was ringing downstairs and Brian was shouting up that it was for them. Three of their friends were in the hall below and ten minutes later another two arrived. "Is there anyone in Belfast you don't know, Josie?" her mother used to ask.

Later, they went to a party where Josie did know everyone, and had known them for most of her life. She danced with Brian for much of the evening. Yes, it certainly was like old times, she agreed, when he made the remark. She felt as if she had never been away. The other life acros the Irish Sea appeared like a mirage. Once she had seen it, now she did not.

"Can I come over and visit you?" asked Brian.

"Why not?" she said.

The days went by quickly. Josie saw all her friends and visited a couple of unmarried aunts of her father's who said that if Josie and her mother wanted to come back to Belfast they were more than willing to share their house and she called on old neighbours, all of whom insisted on bringing out lavish refreshments. She felt as if her stomach must be swimming in tea and she ate so much soda and potato bread and so many cakes that she was sure she would be going home half a stone heavier. When she walked past her old house a lump came up into her throat and she had to bite her lip to steady herself but, at least, she thought, next time it should be easier.

"Why don't you come over for Christmas?" suggested Mrs Magee, on Friday evening, Josie's last evening. "And bring your mother. I'd love to see Rona again."

"Better do what she tells you!" said Brian. "She's used to getting her own way."

"None of your cheek now, Brian Magee!"

"I'd love to come for Christmas, Mrs Magee," said Josie.

"That's settled then," said Mr Magee. "We'll have the biggest turkey in the whole of Belfast!"

Brian and Rachel took Josie to the boat. As she kissed them goodbye she felt her throat tightening uncomfortably.

"I hate goodbyes," she said fiercely.

"It won't be long till Christmas," said Brian. "Two months only."

"Write!" yelled Rachel after her as she went up the gangway.

Josie waved to her friends for some ten minutes after the boat set sail then she put her back to them and to Belfast and went round to the other side of the boat where she leant on the rail. As the boat steamed up the Lough she thought about her visit reliving it in her head and she thought, too, about Brian, with whom she felt so much at ease and with whom she seldom quarrelled. When she 'went over the top', as he called it, he merely laughed. Sometimes that would annoy her in itself but he was good at teasing her out of her annoyance and she would end up laughing with him. They had never had any of the tempestuous scenes like the ones she had had with Rod. Nor the same degree of excitement in meeting and touching either. When she put out her hand to take Rod's she felt as if an electric current sparked between them.

Once they were in the Irish Sea and heading for the English coast she found her thoughts shifting more and more over to Rod, and to her mother and Marge and Emma. She felt suspended between two countries, between two groups of people.

In the morning, wakening after an uncomfortable broken sleep on a chair in the lounge, there was one thought standing out clearly in her mind. And that was that this was Sunday, and tomorrow was Monday. Tomorrow they would appear in court.

Fifteen

The McCulloughs rose long before daylight. Opening the caravan door, putting out her head to smell the morning, Josie saw in the eastern sky the faint line of pink which promised the coming of the day. She was going to miss the sight of the sky and the scent of the sea.

A light had sprung up in the caravan next door. She ran across and tapped on the door and Marge let her in.

"How are you?"

"Fine. And you?"

"All right."

They fell silent. They had already talked out their doubts and fears until there was nothing much left to be said. Marge dressed and together they went to the McCulloughs' caravan to have breakfast.

"Eat up now," insisted Mrs McCullough. "You never know — "

"Where our next meal will be coming from," finished Josie. "Cheer up, Mum, I'll survive! I'll probably only be in for a week." She had told her mother last night that she had decided not to pay the fine and her mother had said it was up to her, to do what she believed to be right.

Josie had told Rod, too, and they had had a row. "I think you're being downright stupid," he had said flatly. "That's because you'd never stick your neck out too far for anything!" she had retaliated. They had stood on the beach facing one another, shouting to be heard above the roll of the waves. "You want to be a martyr." "How dare you say that? How *dare* you?" "What good do you think you're going to do? You'll only be playing at going to prison. You won't really be like the other women." "The whole thing's just a game as far as you're concerned, Rod Lawson, isn't it? You don't even take it seriously." "Of course I take it seriously. All things being equal, I'd prefer *not* to live next door to a nuclear power plant myself." "Oh, so you would, would you? Because you think there just could be an accident? So you admit it! But you won't say so publicly, will you? You won't turn round to Daddy and say so to him." Rod had turned at that point and gone striding off, kicking up sand as he went. She had turned, too, and gone home, saying to the gulls as she climbed the rocks up to the headland, "Blow you, Rod Lawson!"

"So you didn't make up with Rod?" said Marge, as they drank their last cups of tea.

"I can't cope with someone like him. Who won't commit himself."

"Maybe you expect too much of people, Josie," said Mrs McCullough.

That might be, Josie admitted; but that was the way she was.

"Of yourself, too, though, dear."

Josie cleaned her teeth and put the brush and paste into her canvas satchel along with the other things she had packed; changes of underwear, two blouses, a notebook and pen and six books. They could take six books in to prison with them, the solicitor who was to represent them had said. Emma had given her *Emma* by Jane Austen, Marge *The Colour Purple* by Alice Walker, Rod the collected poems of the Scottish poet Norman MacCaig, and to these she had added a book of poetry by the Irish poet Seamus Heaney, *The Golden Notebook* by Doris Lessing and *Women in Love* by D.H. Lawrence. When Mrs Hunter and Emma arrived to drive them to the county town some twenty miles away she was ready to go.

They piled into the car. It was a beautiful winter morning,

frosty and clear, with long rays of pale yellow sunshine lighting up the countryside. It was the kind of morning to enjoy a long walk on the sands. Josie wondered what Rod would be doing.

He was walking on the beach and had been since the sun came up and sent streaks of colour — lemon and pale green and coral pink — across the indigo darkness of the sky. The sand was smooth and unruffled, the sea lapped gently at its edges. The gulls wheeled and called. He felt as if he were the only human being awake on the face of the earth.

How many times had he walked this stretch of beach with Josie? On wild, blustery days and quiet, calm ones like this morning, in the full sun of midday and at the dead of night. He smiled when he remembered their midnight bathe and their frantic search for their clothes.

He had thought she would come walking on the beach this morning, before she went to court, and to prison, for she would go, he knew it, she would not falter and change her mind at the last moment. She burned with a kind of fire when faced with issues that concerned her and she had an insatiable desire to see and experience things for herself. He understood that, although she would never believe it. She didn't really know him. She thought he was a stick-in-the-mud, cautious, self-protective, unwilling to stand up and be counted. He would be counted whenever he was ready to be counted. He had to take his own time. Yet he admired her courage, and her fierceness and impetuosity warmed him like a flame.

It seemed that she would not come now; she must be getting ready to leave. And if he didn't hurry he wouldn't see her. Quickly now, he ran to the rocks and went scrambling up to the caravan park, scraping his hand on some rough barnacles as he went, but not noticing then. He made straight for the McCulloughs' caravan.

He rapped on the door and tugged it. "Josie!" he called. But the door was locked and she was gone. Fool! He cursed himself. Why had he not come sooner? Why had he waited until it was too late? He peered through the windows to make sure there was no one there and saw the bedclothes folded up and the dishes sitting washed on the rack and the drying-up cloth spread over the counter.

"They went off in a big car a few minutes ago," said the old man from the caravan two doors along. His back was bent so that he stood bowed over like a half-shut knife. Josie said that once he had been a trapeze artist.

Rod felt as if his own back were bent too. He sat down on the caravan step.

"You a friend of hers?

Rod nodded.

"She's going to go to prison, her mother tells me, about that silly old power station down the coast. Good for her! I say. We need some more like her with some backbone in them. Show the government they can't walk right over us. You've got to do something to make them take notice. You're not one of them then, lad?"

"No," said Rod, "I'm not one of them." He felt like a conscientious objector who has stayed at home while the others have gone off to the wars. It was honourable enough to object to war, Josie had said when they had discussed it; but it was difficult, the whole business, and not clear cut. Not much seemed clear cut at the moment.

He looked at his watch. It was a quarter to nine. He would be late for his first class but that seemed hardly to matter.

He met Mr Greig in the school corridor.

"Ah, Rod, so you're here today? Half of the sixth form seems to be missing. The Head's none too pleased! Have you seen Josie? Do you know how she is?"

"No, I haven't seen her."

"I'm sure she'll be fine. I wouldn't worry."

Rod found he could not concentrate on mathematics. He kept looking out of the window as if by doing that he might see into the courtroom, and when someone spoke to him he started.

"Are you feeling all right today, Rod?" asked the teacher. She frowned at Rod's hand. "You seem to have cut yourself? You've got blood on your hand."

"It's nothing," said Rod.

At lunchtime he cycled home. His mother was out; it was her day for doing voluntary work at the local cottage hospital. He took some money from the top drawer in his chest and ran for the bus station.

The morning had progressed slowly for the twenty awaiting trial. They sat in an anteroom conversing in quiet voices, making the occasional joke, waiting to be called. The lucky ones were called early.

They had known that they would be called one by one and that it would take time for the court to deal with them all. Their solicitor, whom they would pay with the help of legal aid, said it was likely that they had all been brought up together because they would be expected to plead guilty. Pleas of guilty were processed fast. No witnesses had to take the stand. The magistrate would simply pronounce the fine and wait for the next defendant to be brought in. Conveyor belt justice, said the lawyer. But if one were to plead not guilty then one would be sent back and called again later, probably after lunch.

Seventeen were to plead guilty and get it over quickly; three would plead not guilty — Jack and Phil and Josie. It was only if one made a plea of not guilty that one was entitled to speak in court.

"We've got to speak," said Josie. "To say why we've done it."

"It won't make any difference," said the solicitor, "not as far as the magistrate's concerned, at any rate. And this one's a tough one, I'd better warn you. He's quite capable of wanting to make an example of you, to deter others from having a go themselves. You've not struck it lucky, I'm afraid."

"That can't be helped. But if we can just have our say then maybe the papers will report it."

"And you know that you're liable to be given a prison sentence, Josie, if you don't pay your fine? Since you have a previous conviction."

She nodded. "Yes, I know."

"Josephine Rona McCullough!"

Josie got up and followed the usher along the corridor. She was seventeenth to be called.

She blinked as she came into the light of the courtoom and saw the rows of faces. The public benches were packed with families and friends. She picked out her mother and Mrs Hunter and Emma — they smiled their encouragement at her — and then she looked to her left and saw the magistrate on his bench, watching her.

She took the witness stand, as directed, and the clerk of the court instructed her to raise her right hand and repeat after him, "'I promise to tell the truth, the whole truth . . .'

"'The whole truth'," repeated Josie in a firm, clear voice, "'and nothing but the truth, so help me God.'" She lowered her hand. She felt calm on the outside though, inside, her heart was hammering. Her hands felt moist. She smoothed them against her skirt. She looked very trim and tidy — her mother had seen to that — in her mother's dark blue skirt and a white blouse and her hair tied back with a blue ribbon.

Counsel for the prosecution began his questioning.

"Are you Josephine Rona McCullough?"

"Yes."

"Are you seventeen years of age?"

"Yes."

He checked her address and then the charge was read out: that she, Josephine Rona McCullough, on the — of September had lain in the road outside the nuclear power station and obstructed the entranceway and, on being asked to move, had not complied.

"What do you plead — guilty or not guilty?"

"Not guilty."

There was a small ripple in the court, no more than would be made by a tiny wavelet breaking on the shore and then receding.

"Case deferred. Call the next defendant."

That was all. It couldn't have taken more than a minute. She felt almost cheated. But her time would come later, she reminded herself. She stepped down and followed the usher out of the courtroom back to the waiting room. In the corridor on the way along she crossed with Phil. They touched hands briefly. "Good luck," said Josie.

A few minutes later Phil returned and then Jack was called. When he came back he told them that the court had been adjourned for lunch and they were free to go out until two o'clock. *Free?* It might be the last time for a few days and knowing it, they felt light-headed.

They laughed as they surged along the corridor, Josie in the middle of Jack and Phil, with their arms round her shoulders. Outside on the pavement their supporters were waiting. A cheer was raised which made Mrs McCullough look worried.

"I don't think it's a good idea to appear *too* hilarious," said Jack's father.

They went to a pizza place and packed it out. Josie ate a large pizza, with everything on it that could be had. There was much talking and a great deal of joking about prison cuisine. Emma was quiet.

111

"What's wrong, Em?" asked Josie.

"I'm worried about you. The other women might be violent. And the warders will probably be horrible."

"I'll be O.K."

"We're going to camp outside the prison at the week-end."

"You'll freeze to death. It's November."

"No, we won't," said Marge. "They did it for the Greenham women when they went to prison. We've got heavy sleeping bags and blankets and we'll put polythene on the ground and over the top of us."

It sounded rather like fun, thought Josie, and was sorry she would miss out on it.

The policeman on duty outside the courtroom motioned to Rod to come quietly and admitted him, indicating a vacant seat. Rod subsided into it and recovered his breath. His shirt was sticking to his back. He had run all the way from the bus station.

Josie was in the dock. In the dock! Rod swallowed. He felt sick just to see her sitting there so still and straight. On the witness stand was the police sergeant, the one whom Josie disliked. He was being questioned by the counsel for the prosecution.

"You say that the girl who made the speech was amongst those who lay down in front of the gates?"

"That is correct, sir."

"Do you see her in court?"

"I do."

"Would you please point her out?"

The sergeant looked around the court, letting his eyes travel over the faces in the public gallery before he swung back to Josie. He pointed to her. "That is her there, sir." It gave him pleasure to say that, thought Rod. He sounded triumphant.

The constable who followed him was more wooden and

matter-of-fact and showed no emotion whatsoever. He, too, identified Josie.

Now it was the turn of the counsel for the defense. He rose, giving Josie a small smile of encouragement.

"I wish to call the defendant," he said.

Josie took the stand keeping her head up and her back straight. Rod shifted his head so that he could get a clear view of her. She appeared to be completely in control of herself and she looked so pretty, with her face flushed pink and her eyes sparkling. He knew there would be a sparkle in them even though he was not close enough to see it for himself.

The counsel for the defense said, "You have heard the two previous witnesses identify you as one of the people who lay down on the road. Do you deny that you did?"

"No, I do not."

"Can you explain to us why, if you admit that you did cause an obstruction, that you have pleaded not guilty?"

Josie turned so that she half faced the court. This is the moment she had been waiting for, thought Rod. He leant forward in his seat.

"I pleaded not guilty because I do not believe that I have committed a crime against society. I lay down in the road as a gesture to show that I am opposed to this nuclear power station. I believe that the electricity board will commit a much more serious crime against society if it goes ahead. It could expose us to the possibility of an accident such as they had at Chernobyl."

The magistrate was growing restless; scratched his nose, cleared his throat, pursed his lips. Josie continued, speaking a little more quickly, "Thousands of people do not want this nuclear power station. We consider it to be unnecessary and we fear for the consequences if it is switched on. I believe, in a democracy, that the wishes of the people should be considered. We want another public enquiry. We deserve to have it.

Things have changed, people have changed their minds — since Chernobyl!"

Some of the people in the public benches clapped and the clerk of the court, said "Silence in court!" and the magistrate frowned.

"Thank you, Miss McCullough," said the counsel for the defence and gave way to the prosecuting counsel who was on his feet to cross-examine the witness.

"You are obviously an intelligent young woman capable of both speaking and writing fluently," he began. He spoke smoothly. He smiled. Josie looked guarded. "You must be aware that there are ways of making your opinions known other than by lying in the road and causing an obstruction?"

"Well, yes, but — "

"Were you aware at the time that you were breaking the law when you lay down in the road?"

"Yes."

"That will be all, thank you."

Josie was instructed to stand down and was led back to the dock.

The counsel for the defence summed up briefly, saying: "My client acted out of genuine concern and not at all with the intention of making trouble. She is a young woman of high ideals who sincerely believes that nuclear power poses a real threat to the future of mankind and I would ask you to see her action in that light. Thank you."

The magistrate clasped his hands together on top of the bench and leaned forward. "You speak very eloquently, Miss McCullough, I congratulate you!" He bowed his head. "And I agree with you that the wishes of the people should be considered, but as my learned friend the counsel for the prosecution has indicated, there are other ways of making one's opinions known without resorting to lying in the road and breaking the law and causing a great deal of trouble for our police force which is overstretched as it is. If we were all to lie in the road to make our points the traffic would be brought to a complete standstill!" He paused. If he expected a titter of appreciation from the public benches he did not get it. "The fact remains that you have broken the law and so I have no alternative but to find you guilty." He broke off to turn to the police sergeant. "Is anything known about the defendant?"

"She has a previous conviction, sir, for obstruction."

The magistrate asked, "Would the defence counsel like to say anything about his client?"

"She is a young girl of limited means, sir. She is still at school."

"In that case I impose a fine of fifty pounds with the alternative of fourteen days imprisonment."

Sixteen

Josie lay on the bed in the courtroom cell, waiting. Waiting for something to happen. There would be a lot of waiting ahead, she fancied, and a lot of time to get through. All her possessions, including her books, had been removed from her. Why couldn't they have let her keep her books? What harm would it do if she were to read a novel by Alice Walker or a peom by Seamus Heaney? What was the point in stripping you of everything personal? Did they think that lying on a bare mattress staring at the ceiling would make you repent, see the error of your ways?

Suddenly, keys were rattling in the lock and the door was opening. A policewoman came in. "You're to be allowed to see your mother. So put on your shoes and come with me."

Josie's shoes were standing outside in the corridor, placed neatly side by side where she had been instructed to leave them. She slipped them on and followed the constable along the corridor into a room. Her mother was already there, seated on the edge of a chair. She jumped up at once when she saw Josie.

"Mum!" Josie went into her mother's arms.

"Are you all right, love?"

"I'm fine. Honestly."

"You spoke very well. I was proud of you."

"Thanks! What about Jack and Phil?"

"They were given two weeks community service. They send their love — as does everyone else, Emma, Marge, all of them — and Rod."

"Yes, I saw him there," said Josie. When she had been in

the witness box she had been conscious, the whole time, of his eyes on her. He's come! she'd kept thinking. "Give them all my love. Rod too."

"Time to go, I'm afraid," said the constable, who had remained standing by the door.

"You'll write?"

"Of course I will, Josie love. Every day."

"And I'll try to, if they let me."

They kissed and hugged and then Josie went with the constable. She did not look back.

They proceeded to another room where a male constable sat behind a desk. He produced Josie's bag and together they went through the contents, with him asking her to identify each article.

"Is everything there?"

"Yes," she said, strapping on her watch and seeing that it was four o'clock. It was strange how reassuring it felt to put one's watch back on and to know what time of day it was.

"Would you please sign here then?" He indicated the place on the sheet of paper and she wrote her name.

"Put your coat on now," said the woman, "and come this way."

Once again, Josie went in the wake of the constable along the corridor. The woman kept her shoulders and head very stiff and straight. She obviously didn't believe in saying a word more than was necessary. Josie longed to talk to someone, really talk. To discuss what had happened. What might happen. She wished Marge were with her so that they could have joked together and laughed a little. "Got your ball and chain with you? Don't shuffle now!" She felt as if she were wrapped in a cocoon of silence. And her throat was so dry it ached. Nerves, no doubt. She *was* nervous.

At the end of the corridor another two constables, a man and a woman, waited. Josie was handed over to them. Like a parcel, she thought. She was taken out through a door into the daylight. They were in a yard at the rear of the court and a car was waiting.

Mrs McCullough stood on the courthouse steps surrounded by Josie's friends.

"She seemed all right," she was telling them. "Quite calm."

"Josie's terrifically strong," said Marge.

Mrs McCullough, knowing that there was a limit to everyone's strength, kept silent. She had been reassured after she'd seen Josie but knew she would not be at peace until Josie was free again. When she thought of her *locked up* she had to swallow deeply to quell her nausea.

"Come on, Rona, it's time you went home," said Mrs Hunter, taking her arm. "You've had a hard day too. We'll go back to our place and have a nice hot meal and maybe even a bottle of wine to help keep our spirits up!"

"That would be lovely."

Emma took Mrs McCullough's other arm and the three, accompanied by Marge, walked to the car park. Mrs McCullough, glancing over her shoulder, saw Rod coming a little way behind, alone.

"Would we have room for Rod, do you think?" she asked.

"Of course," said Mrs Hunter. They waited and when Rod was within hailing distance she called out, "Rod, would you like a lift?" He hesitated and she said, "We've got plenty of room. No point in taking the bus."

"Oh, all right," he said. "Thanks very much."

He was quiet on the journey, speaking only when spoken to. He sat on the window side at the back looking out. They dropped him off in the centre of town, at his request. He wanted to walk the rest of the way home, he said. They watched him head down towards the sea.

"It's difficult for him," said Mrs McCullough. "Being on the outside."

"I rather think, too, that he's taking it hard over Josie," said Mrs Hunter.

"They're very close, of course," said Emma.

Josie was handed over by the constables to a warder in Reception.

"This is Josephine McCullough," said the policewoman.

She was expected. The constables left, and as Josie watched them go she felt as if her last link with the outside world was being severed. On the journey the policewoman had got quite chatty. "You'll meet a lot of rough types in there, you know!" she had said. "I hope you realise what you're taking on."

Josie gazed at the warder, though not too obtrusively. She intended to keep as low a profile as possible. Marge had said it wouldn't be easy for her, but confronted with this woman who was taking her bag from her and going through her possessions *again* — this woman who had complete power over her — she felt it would be quite easy. Indeed, it would be difficult to actually feel *high*. She felt subdued, and uneasy in the pit of her stomach.

She identified and acknowledged each object as it came out of her satchel, signed, and was allowed to have everything back except for her notebook and pen.

"You can apply to the governor for writing materials on Mondays."

Josie opened her mouth to protest, then closed it. This is Monday, she had been going to say, and by next Monday there would hardly be any point in applying for anything, since, with remission for good behaviour, she could expect to be released in the middle of the second week.

The warder leafed through the books before finally passing them over. She eyed the titles without expression. She was a stoutly built woman with strong forearms. She wore a short-sleeved white shirt and a navy blue skirt; a whistle and a bunch of keys bristled at her waist.

"Come this way!"

Josie followed the woman out through the door and along the corridor. Corridors with doors, blank doors. All part of the landscape of this world. Josie was taken through one of the doors into a room where another warder waited.

"Go into that cubicle," she said, holding out a gown, "take off your clothes and put this on. And when you've undressed pass out your clothes."

Josie did as she was told. Shivering in spite of the heat of the room, she waited, rubbing the goosepimples on the tops of her arms. The warder searched her clothes, then stepped into the cubicle. She ran her hands down Josie's body without looking into her face.

"Right. You can put your clothes back on."

As she dressed Josie wished she had thought to put a pair of jeans in her bag. Her clothes — a dark blue skirt and a white blouse — were too similar to the prison officers'.

She was instructed again to follow the warder. The next room was full of women. They were sitting at tables eating. As soon as Josie came in they stopped and looked up to look her over, from her feet right up to the dark blue ribbon holding back her hair. One woman with orange hair and black roots began to laugh.

"Looks like school is out."

"Looks like a screw," said the woman beside her. "A screw in training."

Josie felt the heat spreading into her face. How stupid she'd been not to think the clothes busines through further than the court! But then there had been so many other things to think about.

She was given food at a hatch — spam and potatoes and tinned peas and a mug of tea — and told to sit down. She hesitated, then took an empty place beside a girl who looked no older than herself. The girl did not glance sideways, she went on eating with one elbow on the table and one arm up to protect her face. Josie lifted her knife and fork and tried to eat.

"What you in for then?" asked the woman with the orange hair.

"I was protesting about a nuclear power station," said Josie, feeling herself blush again.

"Oh yeah?"

"And I refused to pay the fine."

"Refused? Could you have paid it like?"

Josie swallowed the tiny bit of insipid meat she had put into her mouth. "Well," she said, "yes, I suppose so."

"Why didn't you then?"

How could she say it was a matter of principle? They'd probably laugh. What should she say? They were watching her.

"I didn't pay because I didn't believe I was guilty."

That set them off. They all had a good laugh and even the girl beside her giggled.

"Oh Gawd," said the woman with orange hair. "We've got a right one here. Anyone got a fag?"

Plates were pushed aside, packets were produced and cadging commenced, with those who had cigarettes concealing the contents of their packets so that no one would know exactly how many they had. Everyone lit up except Josie. One woman said she didn't usually smoke, only when she came to prison. "You've got to do something, haven't you?"

A woman across the table held out a cigarette to Josie.

"Thanks a lot, but I don't smoke."

"You're too bleeding good to be true," said the orange-haired woman whose name appeared to be Sal. "Maybe you're a social worker? Sent in in disguise." She laughed and choked on the cigarette smoke and began to cough and had to have her back slapped.

"You're like the Greenham women eh?" said the woman who'd offered Josie the cigarette. "I was in with some of them before. They were great. Always singing. And cheerful."

"Easy to be cheerful when you know you're not in for long," said Sal.

"What you in for then?" asked her neighbour.

"Oh, the usual. Shoplifting." Sal eyed two girls further up the table. They were young, not much older than Josie, and very heavily made up. One was dressed in purple with hair and lips to match, the other had on a black sequinned sweater which had known better times. Half of the sequins were missing. "You two on the game?"

They were both prostitutes. They had stories to tell of their pimps, the men who ran them, how they kept back their money, beat them up, double-crossed them. The one in purple said she'd been shopped by hers, she was sure of it. He'd been busted but not pulled in. She was busted the day after *and* pulled in. She'd kill him when she got out.

All the women had stories to tell, of their appearances in court, their previous sentences, their lives, their children. They were worried about their children who had mostly been taken into care. One woman had been done for non-payment of debts, including her television licence — she didn't *have* the money, she said, she was on Social Security — and as she talked she became very distressed, pulling at her hair, and was told by the others she'd better calm down before the screws returned. Another was in for cheque book fraud. She was twenty-five, had been in prison four times. Her brother was in the business too. He was smart though, had only ever got lifted once. Josie sat silent, listening. The lives of these women were like none other that she had ever come across. They appalled her. Most of them seemed to have come from bad homes, been caught up in crime early and never had the chance to lead a decent life.

"You've not got much to say for yourself," said Sal to the girl on Josie's left hand.

The girl shrugged and took down her arm revealing a huge bruise on her left temple.

"Pimp do that?" asked Sal.

The girl nodded.

Two warders appeared in the doorway. Time to move on again along the corridor. Grumbling, straightening their backs, the women got up and trundled on to another room where they were given their bedding: two sheets, a pillow case and blanket. Carrying that, they were led out again, along yet more corridors, for their medical examinations.

The doctor was a man. Strange in a women's prison, thought Josie, as she sat down in front of him. Any history of suicide? he asked. Drugs? He examined her briefly, let her go. "You're a healthy girl. I'm surprised you should be in here." Josie did not take the trouble to explain. Anyway, she did not want to go around saying, I am not like the others. While she was in here she was the same as they were: locked up, subject to the same rules and restrictions, and indignities.

At last, they were taken to the admissions wing where they would spend the night. In the morning they would finally be assigned to their cells.

There were eight women in Josie's room. She took a top bunk, Sal threw her stuff on the bed beneath her then took from her plastic carrier bag a notebook and pen.

"Anyone want a page?" she asked.

"How did you get that?" said Josie.

"I'm an old hand at all this, dear. I applied to the governor *last* Monday!" She laughed.

Only three women, including Josie, wanted a page. The girl with the bruise had crawled into her bed and was lying with her face to the wall; others said there was no one they wanted to write to.

"Could I have more than one page, do you think?" asked Josie.

"They only let you send one letter and no letter's allowed to be more than a page."

'Dear Mum,' Josie wrote in tiny writing, when it was her turn to borrow the pen, 'I'm in a room with eight women and doing fine . . .'

"If you give it to the screw in the morning," said Sal, "she'll put it in an envelope and send it for you."

They got ready for bed. If they wanted to go to the lavatory they had to bang on the door and a warder came to take them. Josie decided not to clean her teeth at the washbasin in the room, fearing the ridicule of the women.

The lights were extinguished though glimmers of light came in from outside so that the room was not totally dark. Some women tried to go to sleep; others, like Sal, lit more cigarettes and resumed their swapping of tales. Josie watched the red pinpricks glow and fade and glow again. And then the banging and screaming started. It came from further along the corridor.

"Oh, belt up!" said Sal. "It's the ruddy banging that gets me down in this place as much as anything."

The banging went on, at intervals, throughout the night, as did the screaming. Some of the screams were terrifying and made Josie shudder. From time to time she thought she heard someone crying in the room. Was it the girl with the bruise? She thought it might be. Eventually, Sal heaved herself into her bunk and the frame swayed like a ship on the sea. Sal groaned and sighed and then she and the bunks subsided.

Josie pulled the sheet up over her face and settled down to spend her first night in prison.

Seventeen

In the morning they were split up and taken to their cells. The rooms were furnished with a set of bunk beds, one table and one chair, a washbasin, with a cracked mirror above it, and a lavatory, unscreened. As a prisoner of the realm, one could not afford to be prudish. Josie's cell mate was the prostitute with the bruise. Her name was Tracey. That was the only information she would divulge about herself for the first two hours. Josie, heavy-eyed and thick-headed after the disturbed night, lay on her bunk and tried to doze for a while. She had been disappointed not to have been put in a cell with Sal for although Sal might be pretty tough, and perhaps could even be rough at times, she had about her a certain strength that appealed to Josie. She had taken hard knocks in life but she could still laugh. And she knew the ropes about being in prison. She would see you right.

Tracey only knew the ropes by hearsay: this was her first time in. When Josie roused herself and got up to wash her face Tracey was standing by the barred window peering out at the sky. If one looked down one could just see into the bare exercise yard.

"I might be in here for months," muttered Tracey. She was on remand, she said, when Josie questioned her, and apparently one could be in for months awaiting a trial date.

"But that's terrible," said Josie. "What if your sentence turns out to be less than the time you've been in on remand?"

Tracey laughed, a thin bitter little laugh, quite unlike the deep rollicking laugh of Sal. "Do you think they'd let that happen?"

Josie supposed not. She supposed, too, that the courts must be busier in London than they were in the rest of the country. But surely something could be done so that people who hadn't yet been found guilty didn't have to sit in prison for months and months before they were even brought to trial?

"I wouldn't get yourself too worked up about it if I was you," said Tracey. "After all, you don't have to care, do you? What are you in for — ten days or something?"

The door opened and a warder said, "Flowers for you, Josephine."

She held the door open while another warder carried them in. There were masses of flowers. Josie gasped.

"Is your mother a florist then?" said Tracey.

"We'll get you some jars," said the warder.

Josie examined the cards. 'Thinking of you. Lots of love, Mum.' 'You are the greatest. Love, Marge, Emma & co.' 'Warmest wishes, Sheila and John Greig.' "That's my history teacher," said Josie. And the last card said, 'I love you. Rod.' There were three bunches from him, of red, white and pink carnations.

"He your fella?" said Tracey.

"Yes," said Josie. She could not deny it.

The arrival of the flowers had lifted their spirits. Even Tracey was smiling and touching the petals. Together, the two girls put them into the jars and arranged them.

"I love flowers," said Tracey, pressing her face into the pink carnations. "No one'll ever send me any, that's for sure."

"You can share mine." Josie looked at the girl's bruise which was turning purple and yellow. "Why did your pimp do that?"

"It's all part of the game. He's a nasty little sqirt! He said I was keeping money back from him, but I wasn't, honest I wasn't." Tracey suddenly crumpled and began to cry. Josie put a hand tentatively on her shoulder and when it wasn't shrugged off, kept it there.

"What's going on in there?" asked a warder through the slit in the door. Her eyes were visible, that was all.

"Nothing," said Josie. "Tracey's a bit upset but she'll be all right." The warder moved on.

Bit by bit, the story of Tracey's life came out. She'd grown up in the Midlands, her father had died when she was two, her mother remarried and the stepfather used to beat Tracey up, regularly, like every Saturday night after he'd been drinking, and then he began to take advantage of her, sexually. "I told my mum and she said she didn't believe me so she hit me and all. I couldn't stand it, I just couldn't, I didn't know what to do, so I run away." She'd been fourteen then. She came to London, slept rough, hung around places like Earl's Court Tube station and King's Cross and picked up men. "What else could I do? I needed money, I had to eat." She was seventeen now.

"The same age as me!" said Josie. She felt shocked. To think that Tracey had been working as a prostitute for *three* years already! She felt her life had been sheltered, in comparison. "Is this the first time you've been arrested?"

"Oh no. I've been brought in before but previous times I just came up in the court next morning and got fined. They fine you maybe a hundred quid. How're you to get money like that except by going back out on the streets again?"

At lunchtime they were taken to a small dining room which served their wing. There were about fifteen women having lunch. Most of them were on remand and some had been in for nearly a year. Sal was already sitting at a table.

"Hi, there, kid," she said to Josie. "How're you doing then? Screws treating you all right?" She laughed. "How do you like the accommodation? Three star, would you say? Or four?"

They had macaroni cheese (low on cheese), chips and gluey mashed potatoes, with unadorned custard to follow. Josie only managed to swallow a few mouthfuls. School dinners were like *cordon bleu* cooking compared to this.

"You get used to it after the first week," said Sal, lighting a cigarette.

Again, everyone but Josie smoked. They broke up whole cigarettes and made several thin ones out of each, rolling them in fresh papers. Smoking, and all its attendant activities, was one of the main preoccupations: the cadging, rolling, and finally, the few moments spent puffing.

"If we didn't smoke we'd all be in the Muppet House," said Sal. To Josie she explained, "It's where they put the disturbed women. Them that are bonkers."

"They're not all bonkers," said another woman, whose name was Pat. "Some of them just can't cope."

"You can hear them screaming at night," said a woman called Cathy. "And wailing. Like banshees."

Tracey shivered.

Cathy was worried about her children, a boy of six and a girl of seven. She showed Josie their photographs. She talked about them almost non-stop. They'd been taken into care when she was arrested. "God knows when I'll get out of here!" she cried and thumped the table and tea slopped from the cups and ran across the table into the women's laps making them jump up. "God alone knows!"

"You'd better watch it," said Sal, "or they'll cart you off to the Muppet House."

The warder who had been standing at the hatch talking to the woman server came to see what the fuss was about.

"It's all right," said Sal. "Cathy just spilt her tea."

The warder looked as if she didn't believe her and cutting short their lunch break, shepherded them, complaining loudly, back to their cells.

"It must be terrible to be in the Muppet House," said Tracey.

"Don't think about it," said Josie. "They're not going to put you in there."

"How do you know? They can do what they like."

In the middle of the afternoon they were taken down to the yard for half an hour's exercise. This was the highlight of the day and on days that it rained much time was spent standing at cell windows gazing anxiously at the sky and cursing the weather. The yard was enclosed; nothing of the world outside could be seen, although the sound of muted traffic penetrated. The women walked around the circumference of the yard, in twos and threes, and sometimes on their own.

Josie jogged around the yard so that she would make the most of the short break. Her limbs craved exercise; they were used to walking, cycling, running. And when they were back in the cell she began to do some physical jerks, persuading Tracey, who was at first reluctant, to join in. They ended up, breathless, and laughing, on the floor.

"I'll be sore tomorrow," said Tracey. "Haven't done things like that since I left school."

"What's going on in there?" asked the warder who was eyeing them through the slit.

"Nothing," said Josie. "We're just sitting on the floor."

Tracey stuck out her tongue at the door after the warder had moved away. "That was a laugh. Helps fill the time, that's one thing."

"We could play charades", said Josie. "What am I?" She turned her hand, rotating it from the wrist.

"A screw!" cried Tracey, and laughed.

In the evening they had half an hour's association time. This was spent in a sitting room in which there was a television set and a few books, Mills and Boons and some other romances. They should be getting an hour and a half, some of the women complained, but the warders said they were short-staffed.

"You're lucky to be getting any, after the way some of you have been carrying on today."

There had been a lot of banging going on, and someone had had hysterics. She'd been removed to the Muppet House.

There was to be no television tonight, the warder decreed. "Must have her knickers in a twist," said Sal when the warder had gone out and locked them in.

The cigarette rolling got under way. Josie flipped through one or two of the books reading a few lines here and there. 'Gregory was tall with a jutting jaw . . .' '"I love you," he said, "I will always love you, forever and ever . . ."' She had only managed to read a few paragraphs of a novel and one poem in her cell. She and Tracey spent most of the time talking, telling one another about their lives, or playing charades or I Spy. Josie noticed one woman sitting in the corner reading avidly.

"Joy's nuts about those romances," said Pat.

"Must think her dream man's going to come and rescue her," said Sal. "Ride up on a white charger and carry her off. I'd like to see him charging through a line of screws!"

That made them all laugh.

Back in the cell, shut up for the night, Tracey said, "What's your fella like?"

"He's nice," said Josie. "Want to see his photograph?" She had one of him in her bag, as well as a couple of her mother. She'd taken this picture of Rod on the beach not long after they'd started to go around together. His hair was blowing all over the place and he was laughing at that, and at her.

"Do you sleep with him?"

"I haven't yet. I will sometime, I expect."

Tracey sighed. "He looks O.K. He wouldn't beat you up, I don't suppose?"

"Oh no! I wouldn't go out with him if he did."

"Are you going to marry him?"

"I've never even thought about it! I've got far too many other things to do first."

"Once, for a bit, I had a fella that I liked, but it didn't last. Well, how could it? The pimp saw him off."

"Can't you get rid of your pimp?"

Tracey laughed.

"Why don't you just leave his area?"

"I've got to have somewhere to live, don't I?"

Josie desisted. It was no use telling Tracey to find a room — or a caravan. Tracey needed help to sort out her life.

Josie put Rod's picture under her pillow that night when she lay down to sleep. I'm lucky, she thought, as she lay watching the shadows on the ceiling and listening to the banging and the screaming, and I must never forget that.

Eighteen

On Saturday morning Emma and Marge, with Felicity, Trish and Marilyn, set off for London. Some of the other girls had intended to come but were prevented by apprehensive parents. The five travelled by bus. They were well laden. The bus driver grumbled, though good-naturedly, as he coerced their bundles into the luggage space. "Running away from home, are you?"

They took two taxis to the prison. Mrs Hunter had given them the money for the fares. "You can't possibly go on the bus or the Underground with all that stuff."

"Holloway?" repeated the taxi driver, squinting at Marge and Emma in his mirror.

"Yes, thank you," said Marge and smiled back. "The women's prison."

"This do?" he said, stopping at the top of the short driveway that led down to what looked like an administration block. A sign informed them that this was 'H.M. Prison Holloway' and, beyond that, stretched a barrier with another notice above it saying '*STOP*. ALL DRIVERS REPORT TO GATE.'

"This is fine," said Emma.

The driver helped them out with their bags then drove off. They stood on the pavement surrounded by their various bundles, feeling somewhat self-conscious. The outer walls of the prison rose up high and windowless, though there was glass in the administration block.

"I bet we're being observed," murmured Marge, putting her back to the building.

"Imagine being locked up in there!" said Emma.

They were not sure when exactly Josie would be released but they intended to stay until she was. Marge had a week's holiday from the supermarket and the others had decided simply not to return to school.

"What can they do to us?" Emma had said. "The Head might blow a fuse but he'll hardly expel us."

The mood at school was overwhelmingly pro-Josie. If the headmaster *were* to try to expel her — or any of them — he would probably have a revolution on his hands.

The other taxi had drawn up; Felicity, Marilyn and Trish were clambering out.

"At least it's not raining," said Trish, examining the sky. "Not at the moment, anyway." There were clouds about. It would be difficult if it were to rain heavily, or for long, though they did have with them lashings of thick polythene and five striped golf umbrellas.

They chose a site on the pavement near the head of the driveway and laid down, first of all, a heavy ground sheet, then their sleeping mats and sleeping bags which they placed in a row, finally spreading the sheets of polythene over the top.

"There!" said Marge, stepping back to admire their handiwork. "Camp Josie is installed. Except for one thing!"

From her rucksack she unravelled the long banner they had made and, with the help of the others, strung it along the fence.

'JOSIE WE LOVE YOU' it said in red letters against the white cloth. 'YOU MAY PUT BRICK WALLS BETWEEN US BUT YOU WILL NEVER CUT THE BONDS THAT UNITE US'. A friend of Mrs Hunter's, who had been at Greenham and imprisoned in Holloway, had told them that her friends had done that for her.

"I guess they must know we're here?" said Felicity.

. They were soon to find out for sure when a police car arrived and two policemen got out.

"So? What's going on here, then?"

"We're staging a vigil," said Emma, crossing her fingers behind her back. They had heard that sometimes the police would let you stay, sometimes move you on.

"'Josie, we love you'," read one policeman. "What she's done, then?"

"She was protesting about a nuclear power station near us," said Marge. "Well, we all were, Wouldn't you, after what happened at Chernobyl?"

"That's as maybe but you've got to stay within the law."

"What if nobody'll listen to you within the law?" said Emma. "What do you do then?"

They had quite a long chat with the constables. They were young, in their early twenties. Both admitted, in the end, that they weren't fussy about having nuclear power themselves.

"Can we stay?" asked Marge. "We won't be nuisances, honest we won't. And we won't leave litter or anything like that."

It didn't depend on them, they said; they'd have to go back to the station and report in. They drove off. And as soon as they'd gone another car drew up. Inside were a reporter and a photographer. "News travels fast," said Emma. But the girls were happy to tell Josie's story and to pose for photographs in their sleeping bags. And before they did so Felicity brought out the banner from her rucksack which said 'WE SAY NO TO NUCLEAR POWER.' "Make sure that you get *that* in the picture," said Marge.

Fortunately, the press had gone before the police returned. The girls wrapped up the nuclear banner and waited for the verdict. They were to be allowed to stay! In the meantime, at any rate. But there would now have to be a police guard on day and night, which didn't please the constables so much. There were other things they could be doing! they said.

One took up his position a few yards from the campers, the

other went away, returning later to relieve his colleague. The girls settled down to have a picnic but were disturbed by the arrival of another reporter and photographer. People came and went all day. At least half of the passers-by stopped to talk or look at their slogans or take one of the leaflets which they had photocopied and brought with them. The leaflets gave the details of their campaign.

"Write to your M.P.s," the girls urged. "This affects you, too, no matter where you live."

At one point they had more than a dozen people gathered on the pavement. Some spent an hour or two with them helping keep the vigil, others brought along food and hot drinks. One old man brought two blankets which he insisted that they have.

"It's amazing how kind people are," said Marilyn.

They had a shower of rain late afternoon and had to retreat into their shelters, pulling everything under cover with them. Rain drummed on the bright umbrellas and on the pavement in front of them. They felt snug and dry. They were enjoying themselves, they realised, a little guiltily.

"I don't suppose Josie's enjoying herself, do you?" said Trish.

News travelled fast, not only outside the prison, but inside, too. By supper time, Josie had heard that there was an encampment outside the prison gates.

"Five women," said Sal. "Just like they used to do for the Greenham women. Seems it's for you, Josie."

Josie smiled. Good for them! She hung her white shirt out of the window in case they would be able to see it. They had said in their letters that they would be coming. She had had letters from each of them every day, as well as from her mother and Rod, and single letters from dozens of other people, fellow pupils, some teachers, and also a number from men and women in their town whom she had never met. Marge had sent a clipping from the *Gazette*. 'Ironmonger's niece sent to Holloway', it said. That would have raised the blood pressures of the UFO and the Glad Aunt! The warders grumbled when they brought in Josie's mail. "As if we hadn't enough to do without wading through all this stuff!" Prisoners' letters must be read before being handed over.

The news had come at the right time. Josie had been feeling a bit low — it wasn't possible to keep one's spirits up all the time — and Tracey had been in a bad way for much of the day. She'd even been talking about suicide. Joy had tried to cut her wrists the evening before with a blunt knife that she'd managed to smuggle out of the dining room and been taken away to the Muppet house. She already had scars from previous attempts.

"What other way out is there?" Tracey asked Josie. Even when she got out of here she wouldn't exactly be free, would she?

Josie had talked to her for hours, encouraging her to think she could escape from the quagmire she'd got herself into, or been got into. "You don't have to go back to your old life." "No?" "I'll help you when you get out." "What can you do?" "Quite a lot, you'd be suprised! You could stay with my mother and me for a bit." "In your caravan?" "We'll have a house by then." "Oh yeah . . . " Tracey hadn't come out of her cell for supper, had said she wasn't hungry. Josie was worried about her, yet didn't know what else she could do.

"Don't say a word to the screws at any rate," said Sal. "Or they'll have her in the Muppet House before you can say Bob's your uncle!"

"And that really would finish her off."

"'Show me the way to go home'", sang Sal. "'I'm tired and I want to go to bed.'"

Tracey sobbed into her pillow for the first hour after lights out and would not be comforted. And in the middle of the night she got up and began to bang on the door.

"Stop it, Tracey!" cried Josie, leaping at her and dragging her away.

"Leave me alone, leave me alone!" Tracey let out a scream and Josie smacked her hard across the face. Tracey sagged back into her arms like a rag doll.

"I'm sorry, Tracey, but I had to do it." As Josie stroked the girl's hair she felt that she had aged ten years in the last six days.

"What's going on in there?" demanded a voice through the slot in the door.

"Nothing," said Josie wearily.

The five campers were up and about early on Sunday morning. They felt stiff and sore. The night could scarcely have been called peaceful: traffic had died to a trickle but not ceased entirely, and a gang of youths who had collected around them had had to be dispersed by the policeman and replacements whom he called up. That had been unfortunate, and they hoped the police wouldn't use it as an excuse to disperse *them*. It had rained, too, solidly, for more than an hour, and some of the wetness had seeped inside the polythene and penetrated to their sleeping bags.

The morning, though, was bright and sunny. They spread their bags out to dry and did exercises to get their circulation moving. Then they went to a nearby cafe for breakfast; Felicity, Trish and Marilyn going first, and Emma and Marge afterwards.

"Gosh, that coffee's good," said Marge, when she'd drained the cup. They ordered more. They had bacon and eggs and a stack of toast and by the time they'd drunk a third cup of coffee, felt human again, as Marge put it.

"We must take more exercise today, run round the block

137

and things like that," said Emma "or we'll all have rheumatism by Thursday."

Could they survive five nights on the pavement, in wind and rain? But they must, when they thought of what Josie was having to endure.

On their way back, they took a detour round a warren of streets to try to get to the rear of the prison. It was not easy: the area was built up with houses and flats. From some distance off they caught tantalising glimpses of the prison walls and windows, slatted with green bars. A white shirt hung out of one, like a flag. Could it be Josie who had hung it there, as a signal? It might well be, they thought.

Eventually, by going through a muddy car park, they managed to penetrate to the perimeter wall. Cupping their hands, they shouted, as loudly as they could, and until they thought their lungs would burst, "*Josie! Josie! Josie!*" Then they went back to join the others.

The streets had that special Sunday morning quiet to them. A few people passed walking dogs, carrying newspapers. Church bells rang out.

Two women stopped on their way to church. They listened to the girls' story. They were sympathetic. They would say a prayer for Josie, they said.

Soon afterwards, a man came by who was not sympathetic. "Stupid fools! You should all be locked up in there." He raised his clenched fist.

"We're not harming you," said Marge.

"Hush," said Emma.

They knew, of course, that it was a waste of time to talk back when someone was abusive.

"It's not so easy to keep quiet, though, is it?" said Trish.

"You're telling me!" said Marge.

But they felt in good heart. The day promised to be dry and at least they had managed to survive a night. They were not going to let one man with a clenched fist depress them.

The next person to come along the street was carrying a large pack on his back.

"Goodness," said Emma, "it's Rod!"

"Can I join you?" he asked, swinging his rucksack down on to the pavement.

Nineteen

TRACEY began to make cigarettes out of flowers. She had nothing else to smoke and she had to smoke something.

"Try one," she said and Josie did, to humour her. She was doing everything she could to try to keep her in humour. To keep her on balance. But as the days were going by it was becoming more and more difficult. Josie remembered making cigarettes out of flowers with Rachel when they were ten or eleven. Those days seemed a million light years away.

"What am I going to do when you get out, Josie?" asked Tracey. "*What am I going to do?*"

"You'll be all right! I'll come and visit you once a month and I'll write every day. I promise."

"You won't, you'll forget. Once you get outside."

"I won't forget, believe you me! I won't forget any of this."

"No, maybe you won't." Tracey cheered up a little. "People usually forget, but you're different."

They turned, conscious of being observed, and saw eyes at the slit in the doorway. There was one warder they particularly disliked — they called her The Eyes — who was always looking in on them and asking what was going on. She liked to goad them about being only seventeen. "What will the pair of you be like by the time you're eighteen?"

"Is it exercise time?" asked Josie.

"I don't know that your friend deserves to get out. She was making a great racket earlier. It might do her good to cool her heels for a while on her own."

"She was not doing anything," said Josie, speaking slowly and between half-clenched teeth. One thing this place had

140

taught her was to control her temper, though she considered it likely she would explode in one enormous bang when she got outside the gates. "We were playing a game."

"Some game."

"Let her go out, please let her go out!"

"Well, she'd better behave herself, that's all I can say."

So Tracey was allowed to go. She and Josie patrolled the perimeter of the yard together.

"She's got it in for me," said Tracey. "She'll get me when you're gone."

"No, she won't, not if you decide *not* to let her get you. Just keep telling yourself that you won't." Josie stopped and cocked her ear. "Can you hear something, Tracey?" They both listened and heard faintly but distinctly, voices chanting, "Josie! Josie! Josie!" "Sounds like my friends!" Josie clapped her hands and laughed.

"It must be nice to have friends like that."

"Hey, you've got me, haven't you? I'll shout for you when I get out. And I'm going to leave you my books to read."

"They'd be too hard for me."

"Nonsense! Don't keep putting yourself down. There's only one way to go and that's up! Come on, let's have a game of leap-frog! I'll make a back first."

She bent down and Tracey vaulted over. One or two of the other younger women joined in, including a black girl whom Josie often talked to in the yard. Most of the other prisoners were hard on the few black women, even Sal. She'd say to Josie, "I don't know what you bother with that one for."

They didn't want to stop playing when the half-hour was up. It had been fun, while it lasted.

"I wish we could stay out," said Tracey, looking up at the sky, "just for another half hour."

But there was no chance of that. Even Josie now, when she heard the key turning in the door behind them locking them in, had consciously to take hold of herself and not let herself think, *I'm being locked in, I'm trapped inside these four walls, I can't walk out through that door.* Even to walk along an ordinary street with cars and buses thundering past would seem like a fantastic treat. And as for the beach, and the sound of the sea! At night she dreamt that she was running along pale gold sands that stretched on and on until they dwindled into the wide aquamarine sky.

"How many more days have you got?" asked Tracey.

"I don't know," lied Josie, who was counting the days, like everyone else. *If* she got remission for good behaviour — would she be considered to be well behaved or would The Eyes say otherwise? — she should get out on Wednesday morning, or at the latest, Thursday.

Today was Tuesday.

"You might get out tomorrow, mightn't you?"

"I doubt it."

"But you might."

Tracey paced up and down the cell, touching the wall each time with her hand before she turned. She stopped at the washbasin and peered into the cracked mirror distorting her face and rolling her eyes. Then she took off her shoe and whacked the mirror hard sending more and more cracks running and splintering across the glass. Josie dragged her away.

"Don't do things like that, Tracey. Don't give way!"

Tracey sat down on the bed with Josie beside her. "I don't want to give way but I can't help it, I just *can't*." And she began to sob, loud anguished sobs that changed after a few minutes to a low howl. Josie rocked her and tried to soothe her but she went on and on and on.

The door opened. The Eyes stood there, with another two warders at her back. Josie felt a shudder going right through Tracey's body.

"We've come to take you upstairs, Tracey. It's for your own good. Now it would be better for you if you were to co-operate and come quietly with us."

But Tracey would not co-operate, nor would Josie either. "I'm not going to the Muppet House," Tracey screamed and Josie placing herself in front of her, cried, "You're not going to take her, you're not! You'll make her worse if you do."

"You'd better watch or we'll take you too," said The Eyes.

"You try that and I'll make the biggest stink you ever heard when I get out of here!" said Josie, who no longer had her temper on the leash. "I'm saner than you are, and you know it!"

For a moment she thought the warder might strike her and wished that she would for then she would have her in trouble. But The Eyes dropped back and let the other two prison officers come forward to forcibly remove Josie while she herself took hold of Tracey who had now collapsed and was whimpering in a heap. She dragged the girl out in to the corridor.

"Don't let them get to you, Tracey," Josie shouted after her. "Remember to keep a hold of yourself. I'll write — I won't forget, I promise."

The warders released Josie, telling her to quieten down. "Don't *you* start banging and screaming now!" Then they locked her in, alone.

She lay on her bed. No doubt she had scuppered her chances of a remission but she did not care. She boiled with anger. She felt so helpless. But she needn't remain helpless all her life and reminding herself of that, she calmed a little. During the long nerve-wracking nights, when she had lain awake, she had done a lot of thinking, and had come to a decision. She would study law at university. It would be more use than politics and history for then she would have a solid basis from which to help people, and to try to change things. "You want to change the world, Josie," Rod had said once, teasing her. She didn't think she was naive enough to imagine that that was possible but she did believe one could change small parts of it if one tried. And the small parts add up to something bigger in the end.

She was exhausted now and she wept, for Tracey, but she wept quietly, and the warders passing along the corridor thought that, at last, the cell was peaceful.

She was wakened early in the morning by a warder, not The Eyes. She had been alone for the past twelve hours; she had not been allowed out for association time and her supper had been brought to her.

Struggling up, she looked at her watch. It was six. Confused, she said, "Is it time to clean the wing?" Each morning they were given cleaning duties.

"No. You're getting out."

"*Out*?" Josie was now wide awake and sitting bolt upright. "I can't be. You must have made a mistake."

"No, I haven't." This warder was one of the kinder ones. She was younger, too, less hardened. "So get dressed and pack up your stuff."

"They must want rid of me?" Josie grinned and began to haul off her pyjamas and to dress. She was so excited she felt as if she had five thumbs on each hand. She was getting out! *Out*. Was it really possible? She was actually going to walk down a street again! She had lost weight; the skirt hung loosely on her. "I suppose someone like me's a bit of a nuisance to them."

"You could say that. And I think they want rid of the camp at the gate too. It's attracting a lot of attention. There was a television crew round yesterday."

Josie piled up the six books which she had brought and scarcely looked at. "Could you — do you think you could see that Tracey gets these?"

"I will."

"Thanks. And have you a pen I could borrow?" The warder produced a biro and Josie wrote on the inside of the Alice Walker novel, 'Tracey, I won't forget you, not for a second. And I *will* write. Hold on! Lots of love, Josie.'

She picked up her bag and followed the warder along the corridor. The cells were quiet, most women would be dozing at this time of morning, after the usual disturbed night. She had not had the chance to say goodbye to Sal and the others, but that was how it would go in prison, she supposed.

In Reception she went through the same procedure as she had on arrival, but in reverse. She was handed over to another warder, strip-searched, told to dress again, then they went through all her belongings with her identifying each item and signing for them at the end. Finally, her biro and cheap lined notebook were returned to her.

"Why aren't you allowed to take in something to write on?"

"Regulations."

"Who makes the regulations?"

"Not me."

Josie was given a number which she was told she must say at the gate on the way out.

"Why a number? What's wrong with my name? It's O.K., don't tell me — regulations!"

"On your way then! And we hope we won't see you in here again."

You will! said Josie, to herself. But the circumstances would be different.

She was escorted to the gate. She said her number. She was allowed to pass. She was free!

Emerging into the cool air of the morning, she felt, for the first few minutes, totally disorientated, suspended between two worlds. The first car that passed startled her. She hesitated in the prison entranceway, anxious to leave it behind, yet not quite ready to step back into the everyday world. It was as if she had never seen cars and buses before. The sound of the traffic and its speed amazed her. Inside, she had got used to other sounds. That of banging. Of women screaming and crying.

A policeman was watching her with interest. She moved on, and reaching the pavement, saw her friends' encampment. She ran towards it no longer hesitant.

Marge was just surfacing, tousle-headed, bleary-eyed. "Josie!" she cried and within seconds polythene was being threshed aside and arms and legs were appearing and everyone was hugging Josie and they were all laughing, and crying.

At the back of the pavement, Rod waited. Looking up, Josie saw him and went into his arms. He kissed the top of her head and held her tight.

"Did you camp out too?"

"Yes."

"Thank you."

"Are you all right?"

"*I*'m all right," she said. "It's the women back in there who aren't."

"What was it like?" asked Emma.

"That'll take a long time to tell."

"We've got something to tell *you*, Josie," said Marge. "Something good!"

"It couldn't be — !"

"Yes, it is! We heard yesterday. A new public enquiry has been ordered."

They cheered and hugged one another and danced around the pavement and the policeman on duty had to do a little sideways shuffle to avoid them. Josie could scarcely take the news in. She felt she should be more elated. At present all she could feel was slightly stunned. It was only partial victory, of course, and she knew they shouldn't get carried away into thinking they had won outright. For at the end of the enquiry the power station could still be switched on.

"It's great though, isn't it?" said Emma.

Josie nodded. "Yes, it is great. It's been worth it."

"All of it?" asked Rod.

He meant going to prison, too. Josie nodded. "Yes, all of it." And now she must send word to her mother.

"And then we'll have a slap-up breakfast in a nice warm cafe with lots of hot coffee!" said Marge.

Josie laughed at the prospect of hot coffee and fried eggs with toast. Small pleasures had acquired a new appeal.

Rod went with her to the phone box while the others packed up the camp. They walked with their arms round one another's waists and their heads close together.

"Your father won't be so pleased about the enquiry?"

Rod shrugged. "I think it's fair that there should be one. Though I'm still not sure how I feel myself about nuclear power! I suppose I'm one of the don't knows trying to make up my mind."

"But you've shifted, haven't you? Go on, admit it!" she said, but more softly than she might have done before.

"Yes, I've shifted." He smiled.

"It's important to be able to shift."

"I guess you're right." He stopped to kiss her.

It seemed impossible, she thought, that they could ever quarrel again, but she supposed that they would. They could always make up again though, too. As for what the future might hold for them, who could tell? Right now, it didn't matter. The present consumed her.

She went into the phone box; he stood outside watching her through the glass as if he were afraid she might vanish in a puff of smoke. He blew her a kiss. She dialled the Hunters' number and as she stood waiting, smiling at Rod, she thought of Tracey. The world was, indeed, in tatty shape, as she had said to Brian and Rachel, making them laugh, and there was so much that needed to be done that one hardly knew where to start. But the important thing was to make one. That was what her father would have said. The thought of him made her smile, yet she felt a sore tug at her heart strings at the same time. Pleasure and pain seemed often to be intertwined.

"Hello." Mrs Hunter was on the line.

"Hello," said Josie.

"*Josie*! How are you, dear?"

"I'm fine, thank you, Mrs Hunter."

"It's great to hear your voice. Can I give your mother a message?"

"Please. Would you just tell her I'm out — and that I'm coming home?"

Some other books you might enjoy

UNEASY MONEY
Robin F. Brancato

What would you do if you won a fortune? That's what happens when Mike Bronti buys a New Jersey lottery ticket to celebrate his eighteenth birthday. Suddenly, everything looks possible: gifts for his family, treats for his friends, a new car for himself – but things don't work out quite as Mike expects them to. A funny sensitive story about everyone's favourite fantasy.

THE TRICKSTERS
Margaret Mahy

The Hamiltons gather at their holiday house for their customary celebration of midsummer Christmas in New Zealand, but it is to be a Christmas they'll never forget. For the warm, chaotic family atmosphere is chilled by the unexpected arrival of three sinister brothers – the Tricksters.

BREAKING GLASS
Brian Morse

When the Red Army drops its germ bomb on Leicester, the affected zone is sealed off permanently – with Darren and his sister Sally inside it. Immune to the disease which kills Sally, Darren must face alone the incomprehensible hatred of two of the few survivors trapped with him. And the haunting question is: why did Dad betray them?

THREE'S A CROWD
Jennifer Cole

The three Lewis sisters set out to discover just how much fun you can have when your parents are away, and *wowee* do they find it! No housework – no homework – a BIG party – and plenty of boys. Sounds terrific! Hey, who's throwing pizza around and where's Mollie disappeared to with that strange guy . . . ?

MAX ON EARTH
Marilyn Kaye

Strange, golden-haired Max has come to Earth to learn how to behave in a human manner and she picks on young Randi to help her. With a bit of camouflage, they make her look fairly normal. She learns quickly and makes friends – but when it come to understanding emotions, poor Max is at a loss. What on earth makes Randi behave the way she does when handsome, athletic Gary is around?

THE BEST LITTLE GIRL IN THE WORLD
Steven Levenkron

Francesca is five-foot four, pretty, slim and intelligent – at least that's how she appears to the rest of the world. But what she sees when she looks at her reflection is a fat, flabby, grotesque 'monster'. Suddenly, meals become dangerous to her. Food is the enemy, and must be beaten! But what starts as determination soon turns into a frightening obsession – anorexia nervosa – with everyone but her realizing that her life is in danger.

FRANKIE'S HAT
Jan Mark

Three witty pungent stories. Unexpectedly free of her baby on her seventeenth birthday, Frankie goes crazy, or so it seems to her young sister Sonia, in the title story. *Should* someone's mum be climbing on the parapets of bridges, wearing ridiculous hats and playing football?

CAN'T STOP US NOW
Fran Lantz

Can four girls make it in the music business? Reg Barthwaite, pop promoter and manager, knows he's on a winner when he picks C.C., Robin, Gail and Annette to form a new rock band. But soon they discover that making it in the music business isn't that easy, and as Reg becomes ever more insistent that they play on his terms, the girls are forced to question just what they want – fame at any price?

MAKING IT ON OUR OWN
Fran Lantz

It's not long since C.C., Robin, Gail and Annette – Overnight Sensation – were the talk of the music press, but to them that seems like years ago.

Now they're on their own, no manager and no record company, just four girls, their music and lots of determination. Suddenly everything is happening for them. How can they cope with the trauma of leaving home? They've got to find jobs to pay for the band, carry on studying and find time for boyfriends! Can they fit all this in with their practice sessions and plans to cut a demo tape? And what about the elusive record contract?

A GIRL LIKE ABBY
Hadley Irwin

This isn't just another love story. Abby is trapped in her own nightmare world. Often she is 'absent' – not available – pulled far back inside herself in a world to which no one gains admittance. No one except Chip, who is let in just once and discovers her terrible secret . . . and he knows at once that he must do something to help her.

TULKU
Peter Dickinson

The Boxer Rebellion reaches the once peaceful mission settlement in remote China. Theodore escapes and, after great danger, is drawn to a destiny beyond his imagining – in the mysterious gold-domed monastery of Dong Pe, high in the

KILL-A-LOUSE WEEK AND OTHER STORIES
Susan Gregory

The new head arrives at Davenport Secondary just at the beginning of the 'Kill-a-Louse' campaign. Soon the whole school is in uproar . . .

YATESY'S RAP
Jon Blake

It was Ol's idea to play the Christmas concert. His second idea was to get a band together. A most unlikely band it turned out to be. Half of them couldn't play; most of them didn't like each other; and none of them had ever been on a stage. And then Yatesy arrived, with his reputation for being kicked out of several schools for fighting.

URN BURIAL
Robert Westall

When Ralph discovers the mysterious creature buried beneath the ancient cairns high up on the fells, he realizes instinctively that he has discovered something that possesses enormous and terrifying powers, and soon he finds that the earth has become a new battleground in an old conflict of races far superior to man.

AT THE SIGN OF THE DOG AND ROCKET
Jan Mark

When her father slips a disc, school-leaver Lilian Goodwin realizes she's in for a frantic couple of weeks in charge of the family's pub – and the last thing she needs is a rude and condescending temporary bar help like Tom to train.